Why, if she was the mercenary, calculating woman he'd assumed, hadn't she sold Tarika Bay to him?

His lips tightened as he watched her sip her wine, red lips lushly inviting. For a while—okay, since the day they'd met!—he'd been fighting a desire to find excuses for her supposed greed.

He put his fork down on his empty plate. Now he found himself wondering whether her wild abandonment in his arms had been a natural generosity, or a calculating attempt to soften him in case she needed a loan. The thought outraged him for reasons he wasn't prepared to explore right then.

It would be much easier if he could convince himself she was a greedy, amoral sensualist.

Perhaps it was simply that she had enough contradictions in her character to intrigue him. Businesswoman, artist and craftsperson, sensual lover, yet a woman who blushed occasionally and hated it. . .

She had certainly enjoyed making love with him, but did it mean anything to her?

Robyn Donald

THE TEMPTRESS OF TARIKA BAY

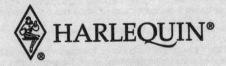

TORONTO • NEW YORK • LONDON
AMSTERDAM • PARIS • SYDNEY • HAMBURG
STOCKHOLM • ATHENS • TOKYO • MILAN • MADRID
PRAGUE • WARSAW • BUDAPEST • AUCKLAND

ISBN 0-373-12336-1

THE TEMPTRESS OF TARIKA BAY

First North American Publication 2003.

Copyright © 2003 by Robyn Donald.

CHAPTER ONE

DRAGGING her gaze away from the polished hide of the bull pacing past her, Morna Vause eyed the spectators at the local Agricultural and Pastoral Show. Tinny music from the sideshows floated across the showgrounds, mingling with the busy hum of New Zealanders having a good time.

In a brittle voice she murmured, 'I'd feel safer if there was more than one strand of wire and a few spectators between that animal and me.'

Cathy Harding grinned. 'I know you're the consummate city slicker, but can you imagine something that big actually running? I bet I can hop faster than its full speed. With your long legs it wouldn't have a hope of getting anywhere near you. Are you bored? Would you like to go home?'

'I'm not in the least bored,' Morna told her honestly. She squinted from beneath the brim of her hat at the cloudless sky, a richer, more mellow blue than summer's brassy brilliance. 'It's autumn—we're supposed to be cooling down.'

'Not in Northland.'

Morna's idle gaze skimmed the crowd, stopping at an arrogantly held head a few yards away. Registering great height—about six inches over six feet—blue-black hair, olive skin, and an air of cool authority, she felt an odd shimmer of awareness, a kind of alteration to the fabric of her life she'd only experienced once before.

And look what that got you, she told herself sternly.

Humiliation and pain and bitter betrayal and a total loss of self-respect...

Physically, this man didn't even look like Glen. Not only was he much taller, his wide shoulders reminded her of the axemen she'd watched demolish tree trunks a few minutes ago. Glen had cherished his urban worldliness, whereas this man looked thoroughly at home in a very rural situation.

Unexpected heat shivered along her nerves. All she could see of the unknown man was one superb cheekbone, a strong nose and an even stronger chin, yet something about his stance—an indefinable aura of complete self-confidence?—goaded her into instant dislike. Glen had had the same—

Mercilessly slamming the door on unwanted memories, Morna fanned herself more vigorously and forced her eyes back to the show ring, where another gleaming mountain of animal was striding ponderously past, dwarfing its handler.

Face lighting up, Cathy exclaimed, 'Oh, look, there's Marty with *our* bull! Nick's so pleased it got Champion of Champions.'

Nick Harding was Cathy's husband and Morna's foster-brother. Morna patted a damp black lock of hair back into her sleek bob and said respectfully, 'It's certainly a splendid beast. Gorgeous.'

Cathy chuckled. 'I wouldn't exactly call them gorgeous, more overwhelming. I saw you admiring them like a veteran cattle fancier over at the pens with Nick.'

'I love those burnished colours.' Frowning, Morna watched another animal approach. 'They make me wonder if I could get that effect in a piece of jewellery. I'd have to use enamel...'

'It intrigues me that you rely on forms and colours from

nature so much. Designing and making jewellery seem such sophisticated skills.'

Wrinkling her nose at the sickly perfume of candyfloss that floated over other, more earthy scents, Morna pointed out, 'The raw materials are very basic. Precious gems and metals are gifts from the earth. And as for sophistication—who could be more sophisticated than Nick? Yet here he is, lord of the manor and thoroughly enjoying it.'

Cathy said cheerfully, 'You know Nick—he digs really deep into anything that interests him. He's enjoying learning about genetics, and the right swear words to use with cattle dogs, and how to put a post in.'

'He never showed any sign of being interested in farming! We were classic city kids—didn't even know where milk came from. And then he turned into an advertising whizzkid in Auckland's best agency...'

Cathy filled in the silence. 'You certainly couldn't get more urban than that.'

'Indeed.' Morna wished she'd kept her mouth shut, but the past that entangled them both had a way of intruding into the present.

From somewhere close behind her, a deep, sensuous rumble of male laughter summoned swift shivers. The big, dark-haired stranger flashed into her mind. She was, she thought angrily, behaving like a hormonal teenager—it probably wasn't the same man, and if it was, so what?

Tilting her hat so that it shaded her face even further, she said abruptly, 'I wish we'd known each other—without Glen.'

'You can't change the past,' Cathy said simply. 'If it hadn't been for him I probably would never have met Nick, and that would be—well, I'm so glad I did. I hope one day you meet someone you can trust.'

Morna shrugged. 'I hope so too.' Not that she expected

it to happen. Ruthlessly she dragged the conversation back onto a previous track. 'I'm impressed at how well Nick fits in. The men at the cattle pens treat him like an equal, yet I believe country people are notoriously hard to please.'

'Nick would fit in anywhere.' As always, Cathy's tone deepened into an enviable combination of love and pride when she spoke of her husband. She sent a quick glance at Morna. 'When I first met you, I wondered if you loved him.'

'I do,' Morna told her equably, 'though not the way you're meaning. I'd lay down my life for him, but as far as I'm concerned he's my brother. He always has been and he always will be.'

Cathy nodded. 'The Two Musketeers—one for both and both for one.' She laughed wryly. 'I was jealous.'

'You had no need to be. We're family. He loves you quite differently.' She met Cathy's eyes and smiled.

'I love him too.' Cathy's fine-featured face glowed.

Morna wondered what it would be like to be as small and delicately beautiful as the woman beside her.

Not that she'd exchange her extra height and strong-boned face, but occasionally she thought it would be...well, interestingly *different* to have a man treat her with the intensely protective love that Nick reserved for his wife.

She moved uncomfortably, transfixed by an itch between her shoulderblades. Someone was watching her with more than ordinary interest—she could feel an intentness that set alarm bells jangling in a primitive warning.

With a swift, mischievous grin Cathy nodded behind her. 'If you want a real lord of the manor, your next-door neighbour Hawke Challenger is the best candidate. He's just got back from Central Africa.'

Morna turned, oddly unsurprised when she caught the eyes of the dark-haired man. Conspicuously light-coloured in his tanned face, they held her gaze for several tense seconds before releasing it to survey the woman speaking to him.

Furious at the cool assessment in that pale scrutiny, she said thickly, 'Is *that* him?'

'That's the owner of Somerville's Reach cattle station,' Cathy told her, adding, 'And the staggeringly chic, exclusive resort at Somerville's Bay, as well as its diabolically difficult golf course.'

To cover the prickle of feverish excitement in her bones, Morna remarked flippantly, 'How could any couple stare into the face of their newborn child and decide to lumber him with such a totally over-the-top name?'

Hawke Challenger chose that moment to smile at the woman beside him.

Morna's heart jumped. Shocked and disturbed, she noted how a brief flash of white teeth and the relaxation of a few muscles around a strong, masculine mouth could turn an impressive mask of force and power into an outrageously handsome face.

A hot flicker of sensation twisted inside her. She was not, she realised, the only woman watching him from behind sunglasses. Such potent male charisma summoned a focused high alert from every woman within range.

Stunned by her reaction, and bleakly resisting, she concentrated on what Cathy was saying.

'I think Hawke Challenger suits him. Anyway, he's not the sort to be swamped by a name, however extravagant. He's got far too much presence.'

'You're completely right,' Morna said, squelching a latent huskiness in her tone. 'Too much—too, *too* macho. He's not in the least what I expected.'

The Challenger man laughed again. Instead of softening that hard buccaneer's face, his amusement seemed sardonic—a match for his slashing profile. He was truly gorgeous, his hard-edged features underpinned by a formidable self-possession that echoed his surname.

Morna made a habit of refusing challenges, except purely business ones, and this one she wasn't going to touch. Chills scudded down her spine, because something in that cool, impervious regard, something in the way he smiled at the woman beside him, reinforced that initial reminder of Glen.

Did Cathy not notice it?

Cathy's eyebrows rose. 'You haven't even met the man, yet you've made up your mind not to like him.'

Clearly *she* liked him. 'He's beautiful,' Morna drawled.

Cathy chuckled. 'Oh, absolutely. So?'

'Beautiful men—apart from Nick, of course—are usually self-absorbed and conceited.' Deliberately she turned away. 'Bet you anything you like that Handsome Challenger is checking out the best-looking women here.'

'You do jaded and worldly so well! I do admire that curl of the lip and the bored tone.' Cathy grinned at her. 'And if he's assessing the best-looking women you've just been elected to that group, because he's keeping an eye on you. Without being obvious, of course—Hawke is never obvious.'

The twining heat in the pit of Morna's stomach tightened into a knot. 'He's probably eyeing you up and envying Nick,' she said uncomfortably, keeping her gaze fixed onto the slow-moving procession of animals filing past.

The younger woman snorted. 'Not Hawke—married

women aren't his style. And why shouldn't he be interested in you? You've got spirit and character written all over your face, and a body to die for. As well as that fabulous skin.'

'Well, thank you—'

Cathy ploughed on, 'Hawke isn't conceited. Dominant, yes, and completely confident—'

Smiling, Morna agreed, 'OK, OK, he's certainly nothing like the agricultural tycoon I'd imagined.'

'What did you think he'd be like?'

'A testy middle-aged man with a weather-beaten face and an unhealthy interest in sheep,' Morna drawled.

Cathy choked back laughter. 'I don't believe that! You must have heard about him.'

'The only locals I've talked to since I moved to Tarika Bay are you and Nick, and the Gorgeous Challenger hasn't come up in the conversation.'

'It's time you started meeting people.' Cathy looked at her with determination. 'We gave you a month to settle in, but from now on I'm going to invite you whenever we entertain, and I expect you to come. You work too hard—you need to play a bit too.'

'I'm a self-employed businesswoman; I have to work hard.'

Besides, she had an old debt to pay off.

At that moment Hawke Challenger looked deliberately at Cathy and smiled. It felt like a betrayal when Cathy's face lit up with a warm response. Morna's lips tightened. Why couldn't her intelligent friend catch that painfully evocative resemblance to Glen?

Not in looks—although Glen had been a good-looking man, he wasn't in the same league as Hawke Challenger. But both men wore an air of arrogant confidence, of complete conviction that they could do what they wanted because of who they were.

Cathy seemed quite blind to it. In a tone that could only be called cheerful she said, 'So now you know you've got a truly fanciable man living right next door.'

'Well, just over the hill,' Morna agreed. She added tautly, 'And I'm certain every time he thinks of Tarika Bay, with its three acres and that lovely little beach, he comes over all acquisitive. Before he died Jacob told me that "the Challenger circus" had approached him a couple of times to sell. Jacob turned each offer down, but I'll bet Hawke Challenger believes he's going to buy it off the estate.'

Cathy said fairly, 'I can understand why Hawke wants it. His land surrounds Tarika Bay.'

'He might want it,' Morna told her with calm determination, 'but he's not going to get it.'

Cathy sighed. 'You've decided to dislike him. I recognise that mulish jut to your jaw!'

'I haven't made up my mind,' Morna said. 'Anyway, it doesn't matter what I think of him. I'm the interloper here, not him. He fits in very well with all these splendid animals: big and well-muscled and seething with testosterone. The colour's right too—I've seen several bulls exactly the same bronze as his hide. And you can take that matchmaking look off your face. He's years younger than I am!'

Cathy returned, 'Turning thirty-four yesterday didn't transform you into a hag overnight. As it happens, he's two years younger than Nick—'

'Which makes him two years younger than me,' Morna interpolated.

Cathy sent a resigned glance skywards. 'Who's counting? Who cares?'

The man they were both watching chose that moment to direct a long, speculative stare at Morna. Hawke Challenger's light eyes duelled with her golden, resentful ones before he lifted one straight black brow in a mocking acknowledgement and turned his attention back to the people with him.

Morna fumed. Over-confident bastard! She'd trained herself not to be intimidated by his type, but it irritated her that while she'd been grateful for the wide brim shadowing her face, he'd held his autocratic head high.

Without expression she commented, 'He certainly doesn't look like your average farmer.'

'He's not—he's the New Zealand equivalent of the landed gentry.'

'I've designed jewellery for some of them,' Morna said thoughtfully. 'They demand quality and they're not afraid to go modern.' She shrugged, adding, 'But, unlike the fanciable Mr Challenger, most of them are pretty weather-beaten. I can see him cutting a swathe through impressionable tourists at his resort—even showing off on a prancing black stallion to match his hair—but I'd be surprised if he does any of the grunt work, either at the resort or on the station.'

'He's really getting to you, isn't he?' Cathy surveyed her curiously. 'He grew up on a family cattle and sheep station on the East Coast, north of Gisborne, so I imagine he's competent on a farm.'

Another trickle of awareness snaked through Morna. 'If he doesn't mind hard work and getting his hands dirty, why did he abandon agriculture to go into tourism?'

'He didn't. He owns land all around New Zealand, mostly agricultural land. Overseas too—he does a lot of travelling. This is where he's settled; his office is in Orewa.'

Interested in spite of herself, Morna nodded. Orewa was a seaside town a few miles away. 'If he's got the whole country to choose from, I wonder why he decided to come up here instead of settling on his ancestral acres.'

'Ask him,' Cathy said smartly. 'Somerville's Reach was practically derelict when he bought it. He poured money into it until he'd whipped it into shape, which provided four new jobs for the district. Then he demolished the old homestead in Somerville's Bay—'

'Barbarian!' Morna interjected on a scornful note.

Cathy returned serenely, 'It was a ruin, and the district's gained lots more jobs from the resort. You won't find anyone here complaining about his development plans. And when Hawke turned the gumlands into a fiendishly tricky golf course, that brought more tourists and yet more employment.' She glanced up at Morna. 'As you well know, because you drive through the golf course twice a day from your little shack to Auckland and back.'

'It's not a shack, it's a bach,' Morna said automatically, turning a fraction to sweep Hawke Challenger's uncompromising features with another rapid glance.

As though he felt it, he lifted his head and once more their eyes met and clashed. His wide sexy mouth—classically chiselled into perfection—lifted at the corners in a smile that held no warmth, nothing but potent sensuality.

A flash of foreboding darkened the day. Lowering her lashes as a shield, Morna scrambled to remember what they were talking about.

Cathy said, 'In your case, bach and shack are synonyms.'

'Baches are New Zealand icons!' Ignoring Cathy's sniff, Morna stressed, 'OK, it's shabby and old, but it's clean and it's comfortable. Although until Jacob's will is probated it's not mine. I'm paying rent to the estate for it.' Her voice turned tart. 'I don't imagine I'll see much of Hawke Challenger—rich, well-connected resort owners might buy jewellery, but they don't socialise with the people who make it.'

She sneaked another glance, only to have Hawke Challenger catch her again. This time he deliberately examined her face, his own coolly judgmental.

Startled colour flamed across her ivory skin and burned through every cell. Bewildered, she tore her eyes free, swallowing as the music and chatter drummed around her.

Cathy's voice broke the spell. 'Minimal rent, I hope.'

'Pretty minimal.' In fact, very minimal. The bach was sturdy, but basic.

'It's great to have you living so close. Nick worries about you.'

'Nick still thinks of me as the kid he used to protect and bully for my own good.' Morna's smile was wry, almost wistful. 'I know I relied shamelessly on him, but I'm over that now.'

'He thinks you're mad to insist on donating Glen's legacy to a charity,' Nick's wife said honestly. 'And so do I. Glen knew he'd treated you badly.'

At twenty-one Morna had fallen head over heels, fathoms deep in love with Glen Spencer, Nick's mentor and the owner of the advertising agency where he'd worked.

Glen had been her first—her only—lover, and she'd been—well, *sinfully* naïve. Certainly stupid! When he'd asked her to live with him she'd ignored Nick's warnings and moved into his opulent apartment. And she'd been lyrically happy, smugly convinced that Glen loved her and that her fierce loyalty was returned.

And then he'd met Cathy, young and beautiful and vulnerable.

Five years of loyal love turned out to mean less than

nothing; brutally pragmatic, Glen dismissed Morna from his bed and his life by dangling the offer of a fully paid course at a prestigious design institution half the world away.

She had swallowed her bitter pride to accept his conscience money, and as soon as she'd been out of the way he'd married Cathy with as much pomp and ceremony as he could command. But Morna had attacked his ego when she'd stubbornly treated the fees as a loan and repaid them, month by month.

Cathy had known none of this, nor that Glen's ruthless rejection of Nick's foster-sister had persuaded Nick to leave his fast-track career at the agency and strike out on his own in the crazy, dangerous, high-octane world of information technology. Glen had been the only person surprised when Nick's cutting intelligence and business skills had catapulted him into huge wealth and international power.

Although Cathy had been married to Glen for four years before his untimely death in an accident, she still didn't understand the way Glen's mind had worked. In his will he'd left Morna the exact amount of the tuition fees, down to the last cent, throwing the money back at her in a final sneering insult.

With these thoughts churning through her head, Morna said to Cathy, 'How did you know about the course fees? I suppose Nick told you.'

'He told me you wouldn't let *him* repay Glen, or lend you the money to do it. Instead you worked as a waitress in nightclubs to get it,' Cathy said, distressed but determined.

'Excellent tips in nightclubs,' Morna said succinctly. 'It wasn't Nick's problem. And I refuse to stay beholden to Glen.'

'At least you used his legacy to set up your shop! But he's dead, Morna—he has been for years. Why repay a dead man by donating most of your income to a charity?'

'I only ever considered it to be a loan.' Morna's voice was cold and sharp, brittle as an icicle.

'You're too stiff-necked and principled for your own good,' Cathy returned doggedly. 'Nick would have been proud to stake you—'

'I know.' Morna's voice gentled. 'Cathy, I'm not going to sacrifice my independence to another man ever again—not even Nick. Using Glen's legacy got the shop off the ground, but if I didn't treat it as a loan I'd always feel—I'd feel that the five years I lived with him were a sort of prostitution. It wasn't like that—not for me.'

Cathy's face softened. 'Of course it wasn't,' she agreed. 'I do understand. It's just—well, it seems such a *waste*—to scrimp and save when you don't have to.'

'What happened to his bequest to you?'

Cathy flushed. 'I use it to support the hospital in Romit,' she admitted.

'So you use it for a hospital in the Coral Sea, and I use it for deprived children here.' Morna's voice gentled. 'Don't worry, and don't let Nick worry. I'm managing.'

'Oh, yes—buying your clothes from second-hand shops, driving around in a car that gives Nick a heart attack whenever he thinks about it, ploughing everything back into the shop—!' Dismayed, Cathy caught herself up. 'I'm sorry. I admire your determination to do what you think is right, but you can overdo independence.'

'Don't be sorry. I know you'd do anything to save Nick a moment's worry.'

'Of course I would,' Cathy said briskly, 'but I'm concerned for your sake too!'

'At least admit I buy my clothes from exclusive charity shops,' Morna said lightly.

Cathy smiled, but her blue eyes revealed a lingering anxiety. 'OK, I'll admit that. Not that it matters—you'd look good in a flour sack.'

'I doubt it.' A grin widened Morna's mouth, but she sobered quickly. 'It's time we all forgot the past and concentrated on the present.'

'That,' Cathy murmured thoughtfully, looking past her, 'would involve concentrating on Hawke Challenger. He's headed this way.'

Morna swung around. He stopped beside her and smiled down, translucent jade-green eyes scanning Morna's face.

Thank heavens for sunglasses!

'Good to see you here, Cathy,' he said, with a smile that sent zings of lightning through Morna's body. Deep, controlled, his intriguing voice was textured by a lazy, untamed note.

Anticipation punched her in the solar plexus and bolted down her spine. It took every shred of will-power to summon a guarded smile as Cathy introduced them. Only good manners drove her to take off her sunglasses and smile briefly at him before retiring behind them again. And no way was she going to shake his hand.

CHAPTER TWO

MORNA VAUSE wasn't traditionally beautiful.

Hawke decided that it didn't matter—skin like warm ivory, eyes the colour of malt whisky and a silky black bob highlighted in dangerous red glints by the sun did enough for her.

And that didn't include her lush, sulky mouth—a sensual incitement he'd watched transform from repose to gamine wickedness in a heady flash.

An interesting situation, Hawke thought; although these women appeared the best of friends, Cathy had once supplanted Morna in Glen Spencer's affections. Hawke didn't gossip, but he'd have had to live in a Trappist monastery to miss knowing that Spencer had flaunted his young trophy mistress until he'd dumped her for an even younger trophy wife.

And he hadn't been close-lipped about the amount that exchange had cost him; Morna Vause had been handsomely rewarded for her years in his bed by the best tuition the world could offer in her chosen field, and a considerable legacy.

Clearly she knew how to manipulate the men in her life to her best advantage.

'How do you do, Mr Challenger?' Each word rang like silver, crisp and impersonal.

'Hawke.'

Morna hesitated before repeating in a flat tone that didn't hide the husky note beneath it, 'Hawke.'

Whisky-coloured eyes, and a voice as rich and complex

19

as the best single malt. 'Morna,' he said laconically. 'A pretty name—Celtic, isn't it? What does it mean?'

Morna forced her lips into a stiff, unnatural smile. Still in that level, unemotional tone, she said, 'Beloved, or so my mother always told me. But then, she got a lot of things wrong.'

Stop behaving like a shrinking violet, she commanded. She was no sweet, shy virgin—in fact she'd never been sweet or shy in her life! Fighting for survival soon demolished any softness in a child.

'Yours is unusual too,' she said. 'Were you born in Hawke's Bay?' She'd only visited that sun-baked province once, but she'd fallen in love with its Art Deco cities and superb vineyards.

Green eyes mocked her. 'No, and although my mother was a Hawke she didn't belong to the family Hawke's Bay was named after,' he told her calmly. 'However, she's the last of her line, and she wanted the name to continue.'

The confident reference to breeding and background scraped across Morna's already sensitised nerves. She'd grown up in poverty and hopelessness without knowing the name of her father.

Hawke watched her. She might think she'd camouflaged her emotions behind those sunglasses, but her square chin, angled with a hint of defiance, told him more than she realised.

As did that tantalising mouth. His hormones growled softly in unexpected need. She had the mouth of a born sensualist—and that was a total contradiction of the little he knew about her.

A second glance revealed the discipline that tucked in the corners of her lips, keeping them under control. Sensualist, certainly, but he suspected her appetites were firmly leashed, an asset to be used rather than a tendency to be indulged.

He wanted her.

So? He'd wanted other women. But not, he thought with the cold logic he used even on his own reactions, with this fierce intensity. And none of them had ever looked at him with such aloof indifference. He smiled, ruthlessly summoning the charm he knew gave him an advantage over most other men.

Her sultry mouth parted for a second before colour swept along her high cheekbones and she compressed her lips into a straight line.

Yes, she too felt that elemental, fiery tug of the senses; controlled she might be, but she was giving off signals like a sunstorm.

In a judicial way he admired her composure when Cathy Harding bridged the tense atmosphere with conversation. Instinctively courteous, he followed Cathy's lead, realising with an elemental satisfaction that Morna Vause wasn't normally as quiet as she was now.

A few minutes later the sound of his name thrust its way through the air.

'Hawke Challenger,' the loudspeaker asked, 'can you come up here and present the prizes now, please? Come on, Hawke, I can see you—'

'I have to go,' he said abruptly. Ignoring the silent woman beside her, he smiled at Cathy. 'I hope we'll be seeing you and your husband at the dinner after the show?'

'Yes, we're going.'

He transferred his gaze to Morna, imprinting the lines of her half-shadowed face on his memory. 'And of course you must come too,' he said politely.

Without waiting for an answer he swung off through

the crowd—a crowd, Morna noted, that separated in front of him like the sea before Moses.

'Well!' Cathy laughed. 'That was more or less the equivalent of a royal invitation.'

'Ha! If he thinks I'm impressed—'

'Get off your high horse,' Cathy interrupted. 'He's going to be your neighbour, so it might be a good way to get to know him.'

'Get to know whom?' Nick asked from behind them.

Cathy turned swiftly, her face lighting up. 'We were talking about Hawke,' she told her husband.

A stab of painful, undiluted envy alarmed Morna. Cathy glowed with a radiance that increased almost to incandescence when Nick tucked her hand into the crook of his elbow. Perhaps one day she'd look at a man with the same naked love that lit Cathy's face now.

But probably not, she thought cynically.

Nick asked, 'What did you think of him?'

Morna watched Hawke Challenger present a large silver cup to a slim woman on a shimmering chestnut horse, her excellent legs revealed by skin-tight jodhpurs. Blonde hair flowed as she removed her helmet and bent to kiss him. The crowd applauded, and when Hawke stepped back he said something that made the woman laugh.

'He's probably gay,' Morna said outrageously.

'If he is, no one's told the actress from that TV show *The Watchers*,' Cathy returned. 'They've just broken up and apparently she's shattered, poor woman.'

Morna didn't want to ask, but the words escaped before she could pen them up. 'How long had they been together?'

'I don't know that they ever lived together, but they must have been an item for six months or so.' Cathy smiled at her husband. 'What do you know about him, darling?'

Nick shrugged broad shoulders. 'Good family, money for generations, rigorous ethical standards. Hawke's no self-absorbed lightweight—he's tough all the way through, and he's got a brilliant business brain. He might have started out with a silver spoon in his mouth, but he's going to end up with the keys to the kingdom. Don't be fooled by the handsome face. If you cross him you can expect to suffer for it.'

Morna dangled her sunglasses from her forefinger and said lightly, 'Thanks for the warning, but I wasn't thinking about crossing him. I wasn't even thinking about having a fling with him, although your wife seems to feel I should at least be considering it.'

Nick glanced at Cathy, who said indignantly, 'All I said was that you work too hard and that it's time you started a social life!' She laughed at Morna's wicked, unrepentant grin and said, 'Oh, all right—I want everyone to be as happy as I am. But I don't think Hawke is the sort of man you have a fling with. He's dangerous.'

Morna slid her sunglasses back onto her nose. 'Dangerous? Surely not. Anyway, I don't play with toy boys; I like maturity in my men.'

'What men?' Cathy shot back. 'In the years I've known you, you haven't gone out with one.' She indicated Hawke Challenger, who'd moved on from the woman with the perfect legs and was now presenting a smaller cup to an immaculately turned out child on a stubby chestnut pony. 'I certainly wouldn't call him immature, or a toy boy. I doubt very much whether he'd be so easy to manage.'

Something torrid and primitive stirred inside Morna.

'All the better reason to stay away from him,' she said casually. 'I don't go looking for trouble.'

The elderly car struggled a bit on the hills, complaining with a couple of coughs as it crested the last one and swung around the worst of an endless series of tight corners.

'There, I knew you could do it,' Morna encouraged it, turning onto a drive that dived steeply down through feathery kanuka trees.

The ancient cattlestop rattled energetically beneath the wheels, its noise transmuting to the crunch of gravel as the car headed towards the slightly seedy, comfortable little house that always made Morna think of a badly cut gem in a perfect setting.

She'd spent until mid-afternoon in the well-equipped workroom behind her shop in Auckland, finishing a commission—transforming a clumsy, inherited diamond necklace into something her client could wear with pride.

Morna had enjoyed both designing and making the piece. Now, with fingers still blackened by the jeweller's rouge she'd used in the final polishing, she was ready to relax in her rented portion of paradise, where ancient trees hung over sand the colour of champagne.

After a hurried trip to the supermarket she'd called in to see the Hardings, drinking coffee with them but refusing Cathy's offer of dinner.

Morna skirted several daunting potholes, wondering if Cathy's delicacy extended to more than her looks. Nick had certainly kept a close eye on his wife at the show yesterday. Morna frowned into the sunlight as the vehicle emerged from the bush, and all thought of her friends vanished.

There, right in front of the bach, lounged a thumping

great Range Rover, a sturdy vehicle that proclaimed its ability to deal with anything a country road could throw at it.

And standing beside the passenger's door as though he had every right to be on her land was Hawke Challenger, tall and formidably confident in the warmth of the late autumn afternoon, hair gleaming blue-black in the sunlight, his stance relaxed yet alert—almost territorial.

Morna's mouth dried. She blinked several times before realising she'd almost driven off the track. Oh, *great*, she thought bitterly, white-knuckled hands clutching the wheel as she steered the car to a halt beside his, switched off the engine and wound down the window.

'Hello,' she said in her most remote tone, resenting that bland green scrutiny.

Morna Vause was ready for war, Hawke saw.

Not that most people would have noticed; a very cool lady, she kept herself under strict control. But, in spite of her steady eyes and aloof expression, he sensed tension vibrating through her like the throbbing of distant drums. Some feral part of him responded with aggressive anticipation.

It took iron will-power to discipline it. This erotic awareness was a weakness.

'You didn't come to the dinner last night,' he said.

A flare of emotion turned her eyes to molten gold. 'You didn't think I would, surely?'

'It might have been a late invitation, but I meant it.'

A fast pulse throbbed at the base of her throat, but although she couldn't hide her involuntary response the only change in her expression was a swift, disbelieving lift of her brows. 'You didn't wait for an acceptance.'

'Because you unsettle me.'

Hawke could tell his frankness startled her. Colour

burned her skin and she looked away, lashes flickering in an oddly ingenuous response for a woman who'd had at least one long-term lover. Was she playing coy?

With more than a hint of acid in her tone, she said, 'It's called attraction—a nice little joke played on us by Mother Nature to make sure the species doesn't die out. It doesn't mean anything and you don't have to do anything about it. If you just ignore it, it will eventually fade away.'

That sounded more like a woman of experience.

He took the two steps across to her door and opened it, standing back to let her get out. She gave him a baffled, glittering glance, but obeyed his unspoken suggestion. Swinging out long, elegant legs clad in black designer jeans, she straightened, her cold defiance at odds with the curvy body revealed by a fitting black top that clung too closely to be a T-shirt. She'd covered it with a black and white striped shirt that hung open so that he could see the firm thrust of her breasts beneath. The shirt-sleeves were pushed up her arms, giving her a jaunty, sporting look.

An interesting set of mixed messages, Hawke decided cynically. He clamped down on an elemental male response and surveyed her composed face with its strongly marked features.

Twenty-four hours hadn't changed his first reaction. He still wanted her, and her stubborn, silent resistance intrigued him as much as it frustrated him. From the time he'd reached six feet and grown into his shoulders, Hawke had been a target.

And although he'd be lying if he said he hadn't enjoyed his lovers, he was fastidious. He'd never made love to anyone he didn't like and respect. Now, confronted by a woman who'd turned obstinate wariness into an art form, he wondered if it was the novelty of her antagonism that hooked him.

Driven by a primitive male imperative, he took a step forward, standing close enough to make it difficult for her to move away from the car, but not so close that she'd feel trapped. He didn't think for a moment that she'd be intimidated.

Nevertheless, the colour faded from her warm ivory skin and her eyes darkened, although they didn't waver.

She wasn't afraid of him, he decided objectively, just very, very cautious. Why? He said, 'Am I forgiven for delivering such a cursory invitation yesterday?'

'Of course,' she said neutrally.

'Then shall we shake to a new beginning?'

For a charged moment she didn't speak, and her hand stayed firmly by her side. When it became obvious that she wasn't going to do any more than deliver a small, dismissive smile he extended his hand, driven to bad manners by an overwhelming urge to force her to acknowledge him.

After a reluctant pause she took it, her strong fingers quivering in his light clasp.

At her touch all Hawke's control disappeared, consumed by sensation. Stunned, he cursed noiselessly as fire hammered him in his most vulnerable places, burning away the shackles his coldly intelligent brain had forged around his sexual appetite.

With painfully sharpened senses he heard the ragged intake of her breath, and watched her breasts tighten against the black top.

No, she wasn't intimidated—she wanted him. Exultant fire burned in his gut and for the first time in his life he understood how a man could lose his head over a woman.

Without thinking he let his other hand come up, lifted

hers, and kissed the fragile skin at the wrist, a primal instinct relishing the rapid thunder of her pulse against his mouth. He felt her fingers splay out in rigid rejection, before miraculously curving along his jaw in a caress that set his body surging.

But she said in a tight, hoarse voice, 'No.'

Hawke's fingers slid along her hand, holding it against his face. He watched the heat drain from her skin and then flood back across her wide cheekbones, softening her mouth into ripeness and provocation.

Through the fog clouding his brain he knew he had to stop this right now. It was far too early—besides, he'd spent the weekend doing informal research on her, and he didn't like what he'd discovered.

Yet it appalled and infuriated him to find out how much will-power it took to release her and step back.

Robbed of strength, Morna staggered, flinching away when his hands shot out to catch her. 'Just leave me alone, all right?' Anger and an odd, creeping dread lent her enough backbone to continue with brittle determination, 'I don't want an affair with you, much less a one-night stand.'

Cruelly he said, 'The feeling is entirely mutual.'

'Good,' she snapped, her head coming up in unspoken challenge.

He went on as though she hadn't spoken, 'What have you got on your hands? Have you been gardening?'

Pierced by an image of a huge bed, of Hawke's burnished bronze skin contrasting erotically with her own, of surrendering to his strength and that wildly sexual charge between them, Morna didn't understand his question at first. She forced her brain to go back and snatch the words rattling around inside it, then sort them into some kind of order. Finally she dragged air into empty lungs and glanced down at the faint stains her scrubbing hadn't removed.

'Jeweller's rouge,' she said gruffly. 'I've been working. Don't worry—it's not transferable, so it won't have stained your hands. Goodbye.'

She swivelled around, leaned into the car and pulled out her bag and the two plastic ones that held her groceries.

Automatically Hawke took the heaviest from her. Because struggling with him would be stupid and undignified she let it go, but positioned the other bag and her handbag in front of her like a shield as she turned towards the house.

Halfway there he said levelly, 'How long do you plan to live here?'

'Until I'm ready to leave,' she said distantly, antagonised all over again. Hawke had no right to ask her what she was doing and when.

Taut silence linked them, humming with unspoken thoughts, forbidden hungers. Warned by an instinct as old as time that this man was incredibly dangerous to her, Morna waited tensely for his next words.

They came at the door to the bach. 'Or until it's sold?'

'Perhaps.' She'd tried for aloofness, but her response came out guarded and cagey.

Of course he noticed. His eyes narrowed, slashing her with knives of pale jade. 'Is it true that Jacob Ward died here only a couple of weeks after you moved in?'

Morna fixed him with a cold stare. Jacob had been an old man with a weak heart, still mourning his only child— a son who'd been killed a couple of years previously. With no other family he'd been ready to go, but his collapse as they'd been drinking coffee had been a shock, and his death a grief.

'Yes,' she said evenly, schooling her face into immobility. 'When he had to go into a nursing home he let me rent the place provided I brought him home once a week.'

Although Hawke said nothing, and she couldn't read any expression in his handsome face, she knew what he was thinking as clearly as if he'd said it.

Her chin came up. She hated the insinuations; they were disrespectful to Jacob, who'd hunted gems around the world before arthritis and a longing for his homeland had driven him back to New Zealand. He'd been lonely—at least until he'd wandered into her shop one day and fascinated Annie, her assistant, into calling Morna out from the workroom.

Like Morna, he'd loved the glittering romance of gems, and he'd had a fund of stories about prospecting; he'd admired her skill with them, and often sat in the workroom watching as she worked. Over time their acquaintance had ripened into friendship, and because he'd had no one else he'd left her Tarika Bay.

So the rumours his legacy had caused—rumours it was obvious Hawke had heard—were hugely distasteful.

Yet he surprised her again. 'If I invite the Hardings, will you come to dinner at the resort tomorrow night?'

Morna met the disturbing challenge in his green eyes. Her stomach contracted as though someone had hit her, but the agitated sensations rioting through her were piercingly carnal. His mouth curved into a smile so loaded with charm she almost buckled; he knew that when he'd kissed her wrist she'd wanted him to kiss her properly...

She saved herself from the snowballing temptation to agree by saying, 'I don't think that would be a good idea.'

'Why not? As it happens, I've already asked the Hardings, and they're coming.'

'They've agreed to go to dinner with you two nights in

a row? Why?' she asked, swift anger almost quenching her reckless excitement. She already knew why—Cathy's decision that she needed a social life! One made with the best of intentions, but Morna felt like prey being remorselessly hunted down.

'Last night was hardly a private dinner,' he drawled. 'Saturday night and Monday night aren't consecutive either. As for why the Hardings agreed—I don't know them all that well, but I can only assume that they don't see an invitation to dinner as an insult.'

Morna had to swallow, because his amused, potent smile sliced through her defences with insulting speed. Glen, she thought desperately, but his memory was fading, dwindling, the lessons she'd learned from him overlaid by the powerful impact of this man's personality.

'Or a threat,' Hawke added mockingly.

'I don't consider you a threat,' she retorted, knowing she'd given him that opportunity.

His eyes glinted beneath their heavy lids. 'I'm not going to ignore the mutual interest we have in each other, but as we're neighbours I'd like to get to know you socially.'

Morna dithered. It was only a dinner...

If she agreed he might be bored with her, and that would be an end to it.

'I'm sure Cathy and Nick will be more than adequate chaperons,' he murmured, the gravelly note in his voice very pronounced as he smiled again.

It was a killer, that smile, and he knew what effect it had. Her heart skidded to a stop and then began to beat again, swift and uneven. 'All right, I'll be there,' she said, regretting her surrender the moment the words left her lips.

Suckered by a million-dollar smile—and a crazy fascination that had smashed across her life, roaring in like a comet from outer space, bent on destruction.

So when she went to dinner tomorrow night, she decided after he'd left, she'd keep in mind the last time she'd felt like this—shooting stars in her stomach, feet not touching the ground, unbearable anticipation.

When she'd first met Glen.

Morna eyed her glass of New Zealand *Riesling* and took another tentative sip. Although they'd finished a superb dinner, she was still on her first drink because she needed to keep her head.

Even now she wasn't going to admit that part of the reason she'd accepted Hawke's invitation was sheer, blatant curiosity—some of which had been satisfied. Over dinner she'd discovered that he actually lived at his small, exclusive and very luxurious resort.

Excellent pickings for a good-looking man here, she thought, trying hard to be cynical. Quite a few eager unattached women were strolling about, not to mention jaded trophy wives. Scattered around the dining room, several of each watched the men at her table with the secret, starving intensity of a dieter tantalised by forbidden food.

Not that she blamed them. Tall, dark and handsome might be a cliché, but men who matched the description were rare—and to see two of them at the same table was probably unique outside Hollywood.

Stick to Hawke, she advised the avid watchers silently. Nick has given his heart.

Yet the thought of Hawke with anyone else summoned a hollow outrage that scared her. Her first instinct had been right—she should have refused to come. If he asked her again she'd turn him down.

Not that she could fault him tonight; he'd been a superb host. She slid a glance sideways to scan his striking profile with unwilling appreciation.

Music drifted into the dining room through double doors, slow and smokily suggestive above the low hum of conversation. Morna's heart began to beat in time to the tune; hastily she put the glass down and got to her feet.

'Excuse me,' she said, and retreated to the cloakroom.

She renewed her lipstick and ran cold water over her wrists before straightening her animal print top, its dramatic contrast of black and white somehow suiting her mood. The black wrap skirt that revealed her legs needed adjustment too, but eventually she had to leave her refuge and set off back to the dining room.

Halfway there she was waylaid by an elderly man Nick had introduced to her at the show.

'Nice to see you again,' he said, seizing her hand and pumping it up and down. 'How did you enjoy your day in the country?'

'I had a great time,' she said, smiling. 'I loved those magnificent cattle of yours—even though I can't remember what breed they are!'

Just outside her field of vision she sensed the approach of another person. She knew who it was; every cell in her body thrummed with a mixture of apprehension and a steamy, elemental excitement.

The voice of the old man as he informed her what esoteric type of cow she'd admired buzzed in her ears.

Her companion broke off to say cheerfully, 'Hello, young Hawke. Didn't take you long to find the best-looking woman in the place, did it?'

CHAPTER THREE

HAWKE grinned, a smile that altered in a thousand subtle ways as he transferred it to Morna. Moving on from respect and comradeship, it somehow transmuted into a molten, masculine appreciation of her femininity that sizzled along her nerves and stopped the breath in her throat.

'I have excellent instincts,' he said modestly. 'I note, however, that it didn't take you long to find her either.'

Through the clamour of fierce awareness Morna heard the other man's snorting laugh. 'I yield my place,' he said.

'Oh, no,' she objected quickly.

But although the older man looked pleased, he said with a knowing twinkle, 'Morna, I've got a good opinion of myself, but I'm certain you'd rather spend time with Hawke than an old codger like me. I'm going to collect a brandy and discuss cattle with Brian over there.'

He smiled at them both and walked away.

Composing her expression, Morna turned to face Hawke. 'Nice place you've got here,' she observed, her voice so bland it was a subtle insult.

Hawke's measuring, dangerous smile disappeared, replaced by cool assessment. 'Thank you.'

The band struck up a new tune, and he offered his arm. 'Cathy and Nick have gone next door to dance. Would you like to?'

The challenge in his voice wasn't blatant, but she heard it. He expected her to refuse.

So she would. 'Not tonight, thank you,' she said politely.

'Then come and have coffee while we wait for them.'

She nodded, and they went together into a room with tables and upholstered chairs arranged around the edges of a small dance floor. While Hawke ordered, Morna kept her eyes on Cathy and Nick; although neither carried their hearts in their faces, they moved in an aura of utter happiness.

Blinking, she looked away. 'What made you decide to build a resort and golf course here?' she queried, scanning the skilfully crafted decor. Casual and comfortable, like the dining room it showcased pale timber, natural fabrics and a palette of neutral colours that combined restraint with a muted luxury to appeal to ultra-sophisticated tastes.

'It's the perfect place,' Hawke told her with the calm confidence that set her teeth on edge. 'Close to Auckland, yet with complete privacy and superb scenery. And the land is almost useless for agriculture—old worked-over kauri swamplands, drained fifty years ago but still only growing scrub.'

Her quick burst of laughter eased the tension. 'There speaketh the farmer,' she said mockingly, glancing up from beneath her lashes. 'If land doesn't produce grass it's a desert.'

Their eyes met, fenced, and clung. Anticipation fizzed through her, glinting in her eyes, softening her mouth.

'I am a farmer,' he agreed, leaning back into his chair and watching her with an intentness that sent kamikaze bumblebees dive-bombing through her bloodstream. 'You've got something against agriculture?'

'Of course not!' Calm down, she commanded. He's just flirting—I'll bet he was born knowing how to do this to susceptible women. 'I like to eat as much as the next person, and without farmers we wouldn't have food.'

Hawke's green eyes darkened, and for some reason every cell in her body stood to attention.

He said evenly, 'Some land should never have been cleared of bush; I have a programme for replanting native trees in appropriate places on all my properties.'

So in his own way he was a conservationist, which irritated her because she didn't want to believe anything good about him.

Before she had time to comment he changed the subject with smooth obliqueness. 'Do you ever wear anything but black and white?'

'No,' she said baldly. If you stuck to basics it made buying in charity shops much simpler. 'Most women in business and the professions choose from a limited range of basic colours. Black and white both suit me so I wear them a lot.'

His brows lifted. 'It's certainly striking.' The intriguing roughness in his voice had been transformed into a taunting purr. 'And I like the animal print—does it indicate a strain of wildness hidden beneath that very controlled exterior?'

Morna resisted the impulse to check that her skirt hadn't fallen away to reveal her legs. 'It indicates that animal prints have been recently fashionable,' she said pleasantly. 'My work satisfies my taste for colour and drama.'

'According to an article I read recently you're making quite a splash with innovative ways of using your raw materials.'

'I like to think so.' Her shoulders squared and she kept her gaze steady.

Hawke said lazily, 'The little I've seen of your work was exquisite.'

Flooded by alarming pleasure, she wondered if he'd bought a piece—for whom? The actress?

He spoilt it by finishing, 'You've come a long way in a very short time.'

Morna stiffened. 'Thank you,' she said with cold formality.

A recent article in the business press had insinuated that her business had been staked by two rich men—Glen and Nick.

Her angry rebuttal of the lie—and, more probably, Nick's cold fury and power—had won a somewhat snide apology, but she had no illusions. Most people who'd read the original article wouldn't have read the apology, so they'd believe the insinuation that she was—to use an old-fashioned term—a gold-digger.

Probably Hawke did too, with his hard green eyes and uncompromising mouth. And for some obscure reason that hurt. Which was a danger signal; she was too susceptible to him.

Taking refuge behind her coffee cup, she watched the dancers with determination until the music stopped and Cathy and Nick came off the floor, still wrapped in that sleek, enviable contentment. Morna eased her long legs sideways to let them past, and gratefully relaxed as the conversation became general.

When Hawke asked Cathy to dance Morna leaned back into her chair, pretending not to notice as they walked out onto the floor.

Hawke and Cathy looked magnificent together—he so tall and protective, she slender and graceful in his arms.

'You can take that look off your face. He's not interested in her,' Nick said calmly.

'I don't care who he's interested in,' Morna said gruffly.

Nick got to his feet and held out his hand. 'Come on.'

As she had so often before, Morna went with him, only realising when she met Hawke's hooded, glinting eyes that she now had no excuse not to dance with him. She said a short, explicit, unladylike word.

'I thought you gave up swearing ten years ago,' Nick remarked.

'I did.' She asked sombrely, 'How did you dare let yourself fall in love?'

'I didn't have any choice.'

Their steps matched perfectly; he and she had learned to dance together. Morna said, 'God, that's scary.'

'At first. What's with you and Hawke?'

'Nothing!'

'But he's hunting?'

Morna shivered. 'That's *so* un-PC! Even if he is, it doesn't mean anything. I'm not good victim material.'

'Is that how you see relationships?' Nick asked quietly.

She shrugged. 'Not all. Not you and Cathy—you make me believe that dreams can come true.'

'They can,' he said with complete conviction. 'You just have to learn to trust.'

'Ah, that's the problem. I don't think I want to.'

'Wanting to is a danger signal,' he said, 'but sometimes you have to take the challenge, no matter how risky it might be.'

They danced in silence for a while, and as the music was winding down Nick glanced across the room again. Dark brows drawing together, he said, 'It's time I took her home.'

Indeed, Cathy's smile was more gallant than eager as Hawke delivered her to her chair. He said something that made her laugh, then straightened when his attention was discreetly attracted by a man who wore effacement like a cloak.

Hawke appeared to ask a quick question. As Morna and Nick came up he nodded and said, 'I'm afraid there's a minor problem. I shouldn't be long.'

When he'd left, Nick asked in a voice Morna had never heard him use before, 'All right?'

'Fine.' Cathy smiled, her lips curving softly, tenderly.

'Nevertheless, we'll go home.'

The look they exchanged ambushed Morna in some unsuspected part of her heart. Small things slotted into place—the orange juice Cathy had drunk all evening, that inner radiance, Nick's enhanced protectiveness...

They were expecting a baby.

Cathy said firmly, 'We can't go home until Hawke comes back.' She directed a laughing look at Morna. 'What do you think of him now?'

'He's still too much,' Morna said succinctly, relieved when Cathy stopped teasing her to discuss the holiday she and Nick were planning in Hawaii.

After ten minutes or so Hawke reappeared, striding across the room with the lithe, expectant grace of a predator. He gave Cathy a keen glance, accepting her thanks for the evening with a smile that tangled Morna's thoughts and drove her to her feet.

'It's time I left too,' she said, skimming the lower half of his handsome face without meeting his eyes. Desperately wrenching her attention away from his sexy mouth, she said, 'It's been a pleasant evening, thank you.'

His eyes narrowed and that beautiful mouth compressed, but the charm was still there when he said, 'I'll walk you to the car park.'

'Oh, you don't need to—'

He slipped a hand beneath her elbow, and to her fury

she found herself following the other two to the doors. Pride insisted she say lightly, 'Nick will protect me from anything nasty in the dark—and I'm certain it's perfectly safe here.'

'Nick has his wife to look after. As for safety—you never know,' Hawke said courteously. 'You could be attacked by a passing seagull.'

She gave a crack of laughter. 'Or a carnivorous crab?'

'Exactly.' He nodded to the doorman and escorted her out into the warm, humid night.

Although stars danced dizzily in the fragrant sky, the darkness pressed against them, stroking across Morna's hot face. She clenched her teeth against the siren song winding through her body, emphasising an anticipation that made her both bold and vulnerable.

She hadn't felt like this when she'd met Glen. This was different—wilder, more tempting, a slow, mesmerising beat of awareness based on starlight and the salty perfume of the sea, and the cloying scent of some flower too close by, and the heady touch of Hawke's hand burning through the thin material of her sleeve.

Gritting her teeth, Morna fought against a seductive, reckless temptation.

Remember what falling in love got you, she reminded herself trenchantly. Five years of what you thought was happiness, followed by betrayal.

No one could accuse her of being a slow learner, so she'd resist with everything she had.

When the red rear lights of the Hardings' car drew away Hawke said, 'Come back inside and dance with me.'

His voice was deep and steady, even slightly amused, but Morna's skin prickled at the sensual heat smouldering through the words.

In spite of the warnings of her common sense, she

wanted more than anything to dance in his arms while music curled around them in lazily erotic expectancy. She wanted it so much she had to force herself to speak, and didn't dare say any more than, 'No.'

'Coward.' Two syllables said with a taunting flick, but they almost demolished her wariness.

'Absolutely,' she said, with such fervour that he laughed, and for a moment she liked him.

Only for a moment, though. Although in the past few hours she'd relished his quick incisive wit, and agreed with much he'd said, he was still a man to be wary of. And she wasn't going to change her mind because he'd listened to her and discussed her point of view when she'd disagreed with him, without losing his temper.

Unlike Glen.

'Where's your car?' Hawke asked.

As she indicated its whereabouts Morna appreciated the fact that he didn't try to persuade her. Of course, it might mean that he didn't really care whether she stayed or not, or that he was sure he'd eventually get what he wanted from her. Whatever that was.

She sent a swift glance his way, her eyes resting for a fraction of a second on that buccaneer's profile. Sex, probably, she thought cynically. That seemed to be what most men wanted, and they weren't too subtle about manipulating the situation to get it.

Hawke opened her car door for her, and once she got behind the wheel he said evenly, 'Sleep well, Morna.'

After a moment's hesitation she replied, 'You too.'

'Goodnight.'

He closed her in with smooth strength, judging the impact to a nicety so that the door didn't slam.

Biting her lip, Morna set the car in motion. 'Goodnight,' she murmured, easing out of the hotel car park. 'And goodbye.'

Of all the words in the English language, *goodbye* had to be the one most laden with emotion.

Back at the bach, she parked and got out, gripped by a strange yearning that had absolutely nothing to do with the man she'd left behind her. 'Nothing at all,' she asserted vigorously to the silent universe.

And if she told herself that often enough she might even come to believe it.

Instead of going inside she walked across the springy grass, halting in the darkness beneath the branches of the massive Norfolk Island pine. Tiny waves made no sound as they eased in and out, and no moreporks called to break the silence, no wind rustled the leaves above her.

She slipped off her shoes and walked down the beach, stopping when her feet reached firm, wet sand. Above her the stars burned tiny erratic signals into the black vault of the sky, diamonds in ebony, unimaginably far away.

The charmed circle Cathy and Nick had constructed would soon be complete. Morna's mouth curved tenderly. A baby! Like a renewal, a gift to the future.

She was delighted for them both, yet even as she fixed her eyes on the small cluster of lights on the other side of the wide estuary and listened to the silence, she shivered with a harsh, wrenching loneliness.

'So?' she stated briskly, heading for the bach. 'Apart from Nick, you've always been alone.'

Even during the years she'd spent with Glen she'd been on her own, although she hadn't realised it; besotted with love, she'd let down her guard and surrendered everything, even her career, until his cruel dismissal shattered every foolish illusion.

In the narrow bathroom off the bedroom she creamed

the cosmetics from her skin, examining herself in the mirror with clinical dispassion. Everything about her face was too strongly marked—nose, eyes, full mouth, square jaw-line. Pride demanded that she dress with chic sophistication, but it was brains and talent and gritty determination that had propelled her from life as a fatherless child in a poverty-stricken suburb of Auckland.

Sometimes though, when she looked in the mirror she saw that child looking back at her.

'Wallowing in self-pity is not your style, so forget it,' she said aloud, turning away to undress.

Hawke seemed to like what he saw...

Halfway through stripping off her silk shirt she stopped, remembering the heat of his lips against her wrist the previous day. And the way her hand had curled against the silken abrasion of his jaw, testing its contours, her fingertips so absurdly sensitive she thought she could feel that slight roughness even now, right down to her toes.

That was why she'd refused to dance with him. In conversation she could use words to keep the distance between them; dancing was too intimate, and she'd be unable to hide the tiny treacheries of body language that would tell him far too much. And perceptive as he was, he'd seen though her—she *was* a coward, afraid of revealing more than she already had.

When he'd kissed her wrist she'd lost control; she couldn't afford to let that happen again, so the forbidden pleasure of dancing in his arms would remain on the 'stupidly dangerous' list.

Suddenly taken over by a yawn, she climbed into the bed she'd placed so that every morning she could pull back the curtains and start each day with the exquisite vista. She'd grown up in squalor, surrounded by the grey tragedy of crumbling dreams; now she lived with a view of beach and water backed by the smooth blue contours of the hills on the far side of the estuary.

She had a career and a future no one could take away from her. She had friends. And she was going to be an aunt! She had all she'd ever wanted.

One emotional entrapment was enough; never again would she follow her mother's example and look for security in a man.

After a restless night she opened the curtains onto the blue and gold freshness of sun and sea and dew-wet grass, of champagne-coloured sand cooled by an overnight tide. A slight autumnal haze silvered the far end of the beach.

Her smile fading, Morna detected the sound of thudding hoof-beats; with a frown she watched a man and a horse coalesce out of the radiant mist. They came down from the hill like some image from the barbaric past, sand spurting from the animal's hooves as the wind of its movement sent tail and mane streaming.

Morna shrank back. The horse was huge, its bronzed hide gleaming like satin. And the man was a brilliant rider, blending seamlessly with the animal so that together they seemed some composite being.

'He can't be...' she breathed, squinting into the brightness outside as her mouth dried and her heart bolted out of control.

No, the rider wasn't naked, although his black shorts barely qualified as clothing. Sunlight poured over him like a blessing, burnishing him bronze. Acutely responsive to the primal beauty of man and beast silhouetted against the dawn sky, Morna watched as they galloped towards the bach.

Just short of it the animal checked, began to ease off its headlong gallop into a more sedate gait. As they came level its rider looked towards the building, and Morna knew he'd seen her. Feverish anticipation shortened her breath.

'Get a hold on yourself!' she muttered.

Once horse and rider had disappeared she hurled back the bedclothes and scrambled into her jeans, adding a sleeveless funnel-necked top and low flat shoes. When the horse appeared again, this time walking sedately along the sand, she was as ready as she could be—hair severely pulled back, face washed, teeth cleaned, and a black enamelled cuff pushed up almost to the elbow of one arm.

In complete armour, she acknowledged with a tight smile, whereas Hawke was only in swimming shorts.

Nerves buzzing, she walked out onto the wide deck and watched as he brought the horse to a halt on the sand a few metres away.

He didn't get down, or say anything, just surveyed her with unreadable eyes. Morna bristled. Talk about a cliché—the landowner out exercising his favourite stallion, looking from a position of dominance down on the trembling peasant girl...

But she was not a peasant girl, and neither was she trembling, although her pulse was erratic.

Angry, because all the cynicism in the world wasn't going to divert the chaotic tide singing through her body, she said with ridiculous formality, 'Good morning.'

'Good morning.' His voice was disturbingly objective. 'How did you sleep?'

'Very well,' she lied. She'd dreamed long, languorous dreams of a silent, invisible man kissing her in the darkness—and the kisses hadn't stopped at her wrists...

The horse moved as though something had irritated it, tossing its head and taking a step backwards. Morna watched nervously, but Hawke controlled the large beast with no apparent effort. Overpowering wasn't a strong enough term for the impact of all that polished skin over a set of coiled muscles earned by years of hard work.

And then there was the horse—more shining hide, more flexing muscles, and the same arrogant air of complete self-confidence. 'Is that a stallion?' she asked sweetly.

'Rajah's a gelding.'

Well, so much for that. She said, 'You should have a whip to crack.'

Hawke shrugged. 'If you need a whip you shouldn't be allowed near a horse. Have you had any experience with them?'

'I grew up in a single-parent family in a state housing area in a poor suburb; horses didn't figure in my life. I just know they're big and they've got minds of their own.' She mimicked his shrug. 'I like this one's colour; the two of you go very nicely together.'

He laughed and her heart clenched in her chest. 'I like that bracelet,' he said. 'Did you make it?'

Absurdly pleased, she said loftily, 'This is a cuff. And yes, I made it.'

His eyes mocked her. 'Cuff, bracelet—they all go around your arm. What are the symbols on it?'

Clearly he had good eyes. 'Snowflakes,' she told him warily.

One dark brow climbed. 'Snowflakes?'

'Why not?' she countered. 'There's nothing symbolic about them—they're pretty and none are alike.' She stepped back and added with a delicate lick of scorn, 'Perhaps you and the horse should go—you might catch cold.'

'Do we disturb you?' he asked smoothly.

'The horse does,' she parried. 'I'm finding all that barely leashed energy and imperious haughtiness a little fulsome.'

Morna flushed at Hawke's laughter as he swung off the animal with lithe confidence and looped the reins over a handy fencepost before starting towards her.

'Hold out your hand,' he commanded.

Colour flamed through Morna's skin. Surely he didn't plan to kiss her again? 'Why?'

He bent and pulled up a handful of grass from the lawn. 'So I can give you this.'

She raised her brows. 'Is this some obscure agricultural ritual?' she drawled.

'If you give it to Rajah he'll be your slave for life. He has two main interests—food and swimming.'

Hawke hadn't intended to stop. He certainly hadn't planned to dismount. But her unapproachable air was a direct challenge, like her ultra-sophisticated chic clothes. So when she took an uncertain step backwards he smiled, and as her eyes dilated that unrepentantly primitive part of him swelled with satisfaction.

'Swimming?' she asked, but she took the grass from his hand.

'Why do you think I'm dressed like this?' And damned inconvenient it was too; his body was altogether too aware of her. Fortunately he was slightly behind her.

Rajah, ever eager, lifted his aristocratic head and took a step towards her, showing his teeth in anticipation. Morna stopped.

'It's all right,' Hawke said, his hand in the small of her back urging her forward. 'Hold the grass on the flat of your palm.'

'Somehow I feel like little Red Riding Hood,' she muttered, but she went with him. 'Oh, Grandma, what enormous teeth you've got...'

He laughed quietly. 'Rajah's not a carnivore. Hold your hand out—yes, like that...'

Although tiny signs told him she wasn't entirely comfortable, she stood her ground while Rajah daintily demolished the grass in her hand.

Hawke felt an odd pride. 'You can stroke his nose if you'd like to.'

She ran a very tentative hand up the horse's long nose; Rajah snorted before politely bending his head to indicate silently that he preferred to be scratched between the ears. Hawke watched Morna's long fingers move lightly against the animal's polished coat and wondered what they'd feel like on his skin.

Too good, he thought, feeling his body stir. He said, 'Maybe you think *I'm* the wolf,' and cursed the raw note in the words.

Only her fingers moved against the horse's coat. They stilled, and when Rajah tossed his head in displeasure she stepped away from the animal and said, 'I certainly wasn't referring to Rajah.'

Hawke considered himself long past the age of responding to reckless dares, yet when she turned her head to meet his eyes with a cool, unsubtle challenge he gave up trying to ignore the effect her slim, sleek body was having on him.

CHAPTER FOUR

'WOLVES don't have a good name,' Hawke said, catching her wrist and pulling her towards him. 'Unfair, I've always thought. I rather admire them.'

Morna came into his arms as though she belonged there, tautly eager, her face lifting so that she could survey him, tawny eyes huge and dark, soft lips parted.

Hawke gave a harsh sigh of pure male satisfaction and kissed her name onto her lips, arms curving around her back to hold her against his big, savagely aroused body.

Conquered by an astonishing, fiercely sexual enchantment, Morna kissed him back, her mouth moulding to his, exulting at the bold evidence of his desire. Nothing, she thought dazedly, had prepared her for such a wholesale annihilation of everything but the compulsion to follow this dangerous path to ecstasy.

Crushed against him, catching fire from his heat, she opened her mouth to the demand of his, shuddering with incandescent pleasure as he made himself master of the sensitive interior.

Raw passion drove through her, scattering her thoughts like sparks in a firestorm. Glorying in it, she surrendered completely, inhaling his scent, hot and salty and completely male, and the feel of him beneath her hands, solid and sleek and powerful.

Hawke lifted his head and said her name against her throat, and she smiled, her lips tender from his kisses, and forced up heavy eyelids. He was leaning back against a post, supporting her while his mouth found the acutely sensitive place where her neck joined her shoulder. When she groaned he introduced her to the sharp sensation of his teeth on her earlobe, and his hand slid to the soft mound of one breast, cupping it.

Sheer ravishment made her gasp and open her eyes into the sun. The radiance pierced her like a sword, as keen as the pleasure of holding and kissing Hawke.

He said harshly, 'You know where this is going, don't you?'

Morna came crashing back to earth, her desperate desire suddenly replaced by shock and shame. Yes, she knew; this kiss had only one end in sight.

She was letting a dominating stranger kiss her, gentle her into submission. Already she'd touched him with spurious, dangerous intimacy, her hands lingering on his skin, the inner passages of her body heating and moistening in preparation.

In a voice she barely recognised, she said, 'Nowhere.'

Clamping her eyes shut, she swallowed to ease the tightness in her throat. It took every scrap of will she possessed to say, 'Let me go.'

Instead, he held her away. Shivering at the rush of cool air onto her sensitive skin, she had to force up her lashes and stare at his face, hard and dark and compelling in the morning sunlight. Mouth throbbing under his narrowed, scornful survey, she flushed.

'If you mean that,' he said levelly, contempt rasping through the words, 'there's an easy way to make it stick. Freeze me off. Looking at you makes me hard; touching you lets loose more than a few demons; but I'm not a rapist.'

She pressed her lips together, holding back the accusation that he had started it.

Her shameless, eager response had given him tacit permission to take what he wanted. Huskily she said, 'It seems I'm no more immune to your considerable charms than—anyone else. I don't want this to go any further.'

Hawke dropped his arms and stepped back, leaving her cold and alone in the fresh morning air. But safe, she reminded herself.

She wrenched away and swung on her heel. Refusing to trust her voice or her brain, she clamped her mouth tightly shut and walked into the bach with her head held so high her shoulders ached. Awash with frustration and adrenalin, she heard him click his tongue at the horse.

Once she'd heard the muffled thud of hooves she allowed her head to turn—just enough so she could see man and animal pacing away down the beach. As though Hawke knew she couldn't resist that reluctant final survey he lifted a hand in a mocking salute.

'Arrogant snob,' she muttered, angry with herself for stealing that peek—and even more angry with him for being so confident she'd do it.

'Arrogant, overbearing snob,' she said defiantly, slamming the door of the bach behind her.

And dynamic and disturbing and forbidden...

Her cellphone chirruped impertinently. 'Are you on your way to work?' Cathy asked cheerfully.

'Not yet.' Morna glanced at her watch. 'But I have to run.'

'OK, so I won't delay you by gossiping about last night. Would you like to come to lunch on Saturday? It's going to be a very informal neighbourhood get-together before Nick and I head off to the fleshpots of Hawaii.'

'I'd love to,' Morna said. Quite apart from enjoying their company, lunch with the Hardings would stop her from thinking about Hawke Challenger.

And so would work. She snatched a piece of bread from

the fridge, slathered it with peanut butter and headed out
to the car, munching as she went.

Fortunately it was a busy week. She was commissioned
to design a ring set for a newly engaged couple, neither
of whom had any idea of what they wanted, so there were
lengthy, irritating interviews followed by hours spent pro-
ducing working drawings. The couple admired each design extravagantly, only for one of them to reject it five
minutes later.

'Sometimes,' she said dourly to her assistant Annie as
the arguing pair walked out of the shop, 'I think I should
have taken courses in psychology. I doubt if they'll ever
get to the altar.'

But there were other, more profitable commissions, and
she was asked to mount a showcase on one of the big
cruise liners that called into Port Auckland.

Each night she came home in the dark and slept
heavily, until her sleep was broken by dreams that slowly
became more and more erotic. The man's face was
shrouded by darkness, but she knew who he was. And she
knew what he represented—the loss of her integrity in
another relationship based on nothing more stable than the
shifting, perilous sands of passion.

So when she looked up from a lounger at the Hardings'
place to see Hawke descend the steps to the pool with
Nick, she felt stupidly betrayed. Her first instinct was to
cower behind the scanty safety of her sunglasses, desperately hoping she looked poised and *soignée*.

Vain hope! Although her plain black swimsuit was con-
servatively cut, the large black and white shawl she'd tied
at the hip revealed far too much of her long legs to
Hawke's ironic glance.

If she'd known he was coming she'd have worn trousers and a shirt. And a veil? she asked herself scathingly, pinning a small distant smile to her face.

'Hello, Hawke,' she said in her most serene, uninvolved voice.

He inclined his head towards her, eyes remotely speculative. 'Morna.'

Was he remembering the ferocious intensity of those kisses?

Morna certainly was. Her busy week hadn't blotted out the taste of Hawke's mouth on hers, and the white-hot fever it had summoned—a fever that hadn't died. Even now her skin tightened as humiliating arousal twisted deep inside her.

To her chagrin he sat down in the empty chair beside her. Although he was far too sophisticated to openly admire her sleek form on the lounger, she felt helpless and foolishly vulnerable.

He knew, too. She resented the cool gleam of amusement in his smile even as her body responded to his overpowering presence. Worst of all though, even more dangerous than the hidden rills of excitement pulsing through her, was an alarming feeling of completion, of safeness.

Safe? Because of Hawke Challenger? She had to be going out of her mind.

Anger at her ridiculous response drove her to swing her legs over the side of the lounger and sit up. Pulling off her headband, she shook her head so that the black fall of hair provided some shelter for her face.

And then, deliberately, she let her gaze assess his well-cut shirt and the trousers that hugged his narrow hips and heavily muscled thighs.

He suffered her catalogue of his assets with a cool smile and a disturbing gleam in his pale eyes. When she looked away he leaned forward and said outrageously, 'Nice legs.'

Shock froze her tongue for a few seconds, until she flashed, 'I like yours too. You must work out religiously.'

His smile was bland. 'Farming is good for developing strength.'

Fortunately several new arrivals appeared at the top of the steps. The slight resultant fuss of introductions eased the tension knotting Morna's stomach, especially when an extremely pretty girl of about sixteen took one look at Hawke and sighed, 'Oh, do you mind if I fall in love with you?'

'How could I mind?' he said with a smile that probably curled the toes of every woman who saw it. 'I'm almost old enough to be your father, but don't let that worry you. Everyone's entitled to a heart-breaking, unrequited love affair with an unsuitable person at least once before they're twenty.'

After a wide-eyed stare the girl burst into laughter, before taking his reply as an invitation to test her skill at flirtation.

Covertly watching them, Morna was oddly touched by Hawke's understanding of adolescence; he treated the girl with a charm that skilfully combined a suitable appreciation for her budding womanhood with a definite hands-off position.

So he was good with young people. Why should that make her edgy?

Because she didn't want him to be kind, or thoughtful, or sensitive. It would be too easy to add such qualities to the ones she already liked about him—his ability to argue without trying to make her feel a fool and his cool, incisive intelligence. Combined with a subtle sense of humour, they made for a dangerously compelling man.

Restlessly looking around, she saw Cathy turn white; Morna sprang up as the younger woman made for a chair with the blind concentration of someone about to faint. Drawn by invisible bonds, Nick glanced around, immediately abandoning the group he was with to go across to his wife and crouch beside the chair.

Morna circulated inconspicuously until she reached them both. 'All right?' she asked, scrutinising her hostess, whose small face was still too pale.

Smiling weakly, Cathy fanned herself with her hand. 'I'm fine. You were right last weekend at the show—it is too hot for autumn. It's so sheltered here I felt a bit peculiar, but the breeze has chased it away.'

And indeed the colour was coming back into her skin. After a glance at Nick, Morna asked bluntly, 'Do you want me to get rid of these people?'

'Don't you dare.' Cathy looked at her husband. 'Truly, both of you, I'm perfectly all right now.'

Nick stood up and said in a tone that lifted the hair on Morna's skin, 'Take it easy. One more little episode like that and *I'll* send them on their way.'

'You fuss—'

'How can I not?' Nick asked in a tone that made Morna feel like an intruder.

From then on she appointed herself as secondary hostess, grateful for the excuse to stay well away from Hawke.

From across the pool Morna saw him introduce his youthful admirer to a young man much closer to her own age. The three chatted together for a few minutes until Hawke left. Later she noticed him with another woman, one using blatant tactics to keep his attention.

Pretty obvious, that lash-flicking and lip-licking, the manicured fingers playing with the skilfully blonded hair,

Morna thought snidely, and then felt ashamed of her unusual malice.

Hawke chose that second to glance up. For tense moments they stared at each other, until Morna turned away, cheeks hot and stomach churning. There had been something—something like a claim—in his ironic green gaze, as though he'd branded her.

God, how melodramatic could you get?

Cathy's colouring stayed stable during the relaxed lunch beneath a wide, shady tree. While Nick kept a close watch on his wife, Morna steered her own gaze resolutely away from the far end of the table.

She realised with a jolt of awareness that since Hawke had arrived she'd known exactly where he was and who he was with.

Later, negotiating the winding road home, she warned herself not to be an idiot. Of course he hadn't staked an unspoken claim—that was so outrageous she could dismiss the idea right now and never think of it again.

Hawke hadn't come near her for the rest of the afternoon, and that uncomfortable sense of being marked out from the group was just another indication of her newborn tendency to dramatise.

'I want Hawke Challenger,' she said aloud, stressing his name with as much sarcasm as she could inject into her voice.

Just as she'd wanted Glen. She seemed to be an impetuous lover, falling into instant lust at first sight. But her experience with Glen had taught her that lust wasn't love; she'd set up a straw man, believing in her illusions with a desperate faith that deserved a better cause. Glen had shown her that she couldn't trust herself to choose wisely.

So she'd chosen no others, keeping herself safe and aloof.

And she didn't dare give in to this wildfire hunger for a man she didn't know. She'd probably chosen the much older Glen, she thought with painful honesty, because she'd never known a father. Hawke was different. Instinct warned her that if she gave in to her desire for him she wouldn't be able to maintain the control she so desperately needed.

She drove sedately past the turn-off to the resort, squinting behind her dark glasses when the sun beat in through the side window, relieved when the graceful canopy of kanuka trees blocked out the probing rays.

As she switched off the engine a flash of movement in the rear-vision mirror caught her eye. A car—a Range Rover—had followed her down and was now drawing up beside hers.

Moisture dampened her temples. Hawke was the last person she wanted to see, yet the prospect of his arrival shortened her breath and sent her pulse into an uneven gallop.

She got out, but kept her car between her and the intruder, and watched warily while Hawke strode with lethal grace over the grass. His physical dominance assailed her like a weapon, chipping away at the defences she'd so painfully constructed.

'What do you want?' Her voice barely made it past the constriction in her throat.

A gaze as pale and cold as winter ice scanned her face. 'To find out why you didn't tell me that you now own Tarika Bay.'

'I didn't tell you because it's none of your business,' Morna told him stonily. 'And because I don't own it.'

Hawke said with contemptuous clarity, 'Are you denying that Jacob Ward left it to you?'

'No,' she said angrily. 'But it's not mine yet.'

'It will be once the probate formalities are dealt with.' Impatience tinged his voice, and at her reluctant nod he cut straight to the chase. 'When you get possession I'll pay you considerably more for it than the valuation.'

Chin lifting to an aggressive angle, Morna returned, 'I won't be selling.'

'Why?'

'Because Jacob didn't want me to.'

She'd tried to persuade the old man to leave it to one of the organisations set up to protect land from development, but none of them considered Tarika Bay to have natural features worth covenanting. Beautiful beaches were common in the north.

'I presume he had a reason?' When she hesitated he said inflexibly, 'Well?'

She straightened her spine. 'He disliked what you were doing here. You turned Somerville's Bay into a resort, and the gumlands into a golf course for rich people.'

'Plenty of far-from-rich locals play here,' he cut in. 'And plenty of locals earn their living from the development.'

'I know,' Morna said quietly. 'But he loved it just the way it was. He realised you'd probably try to buy it after he died, and he wanted to safeguard it—left the way it is. Natural,' she added as an afterthought.

One sable brow lifted in sardonic disbelief. 'Natural? Then you'll have to demolish the bach and cut down the Norfolk Island pine. And get rid of every runner of grass, and the hibiscuses, not to mention the Fijian fire bushes and the century trees.'

'I'm sure you know what he meant,' she returned coldly.

'Did you agree with him?'

This time Morna's hesitation lasted only a second. 'I intend to respect his wishes.'

She didn't agree with Jacob, who'd pined for what he'd believed to be the untouched country of his youth, but Hawke would probably see any admission as a sign of weakness and apply more pressure.

And she certainly wasn't going to tell him of her plans for the land. The charity that received her weekly instalments of Glen's legacy sent underprivileged children on holidays their parents couldn't afford. Tarika Bay would be perfect for a camp.

When she didn't elaborate Hawke said with cold irony, 'Wait until you get your first rates assessment.'

Morna frowned. 'Why?'

'Coastal land is expensive. Why do you think so many landowners have sold their land for housing? When I bought the place the rates were draining every bit of profit from Somerville's Reach. It was either development or subdivision. Unless your business is extremely profitable, or you have another source of income, Tarika Bay will be a massive drain on your resources.'

Stupid, but she hadn't even thought about property rates!

When she remained silent, he asked, 'Was Jacob Ward some connection of yours?'

'No,' she said baldly, thrown by the abrupt change of subject. She clarified her answer by stating, 'We were friends.'

Again that disbelieving brow rose with deadly effectiveness. Hawke said silkily, 'I'm prepared to pay as much as the land is worth, but don't think of holding me to ransom, Morna. I won't offer a cent more than its value to me.'

She resisted the urge to cross her wrists over her chest and run her palms down her suddenly chilly arms. 'I'm not selling it, so playing the heavy won't get you anywhere.'

'I'll object to any development,' he said, his dispassionate tone at variance with the uncompromising green ice in his gaze.

'I don't plan any,' she returned, her voice crisp and curt. Sheer pride, arrogant and stiff-necked, prodded her into finishing, 'Not that your threats would make me change my mind!'

'I can make sure you don't sell it to anyone else,' he said calmly.

Her eyelashes flew up. Stark, uncompromising determination hardened his overly handsome face, turning him into a formidable enemy. Some fragile, barely born emotion died inside Morna. She asked curtly, 'How?'

'The bach is almost a ruin, so any buyer will plan development, even if they only mean to build a better house. But no developer is going to pick a fight with me. You might as well sell to me—you're not likely to get a better offer.'

'I'm not selling to anyone,' she said, her voice as determined as the darkening eyes that met his so steadily. 'And if my being here annoys you so much, just ignore me.'

'I can't,' he said tightly, adding with a cold conviction, 'any more than you can ignore me.'

'Do you think I can't resist you?' she flashed.

He didn't answer. Not in speech, anyway. Had she used her sultry, disturbing sensuality on old Jacob Ward before he died and left her his bach, his three acres and one of

Northland's most beautiful beaches? A white-hot wave of primitive anger astonished and disgusted him.

Furious with himself for losing control, and with her for being so damned stubborn, he rested the tip of his index finger on the pulse thudding in her throat.

With an insolent smile he watched the shamed droop of lashes over her dilated eyes, the quick withdrawal.

And then the angry resentment.

He understood that resentment—it corroded his emotions too. Why could this acquisitive woman, with her suspect moral code, almost override the restraint of a lifetime?

'I know you'd try,' he said, the contempt in his tone directed at himself. Dropping his hand, he finished, 'So would I. But if you keep living here it's going to happen. Inevitable as winter, violent as a bushfire.'

And as destructive, Morna thought, making a heroic effort to withstand his fierce magnetism. Sex with Hawke would be wild and hot, burning common sense and self-esteem in a bonfire of passion. Yet in spite of the warning her body leapt into life at the thought of it—and if her dreams were any indication she spent her sleeping hours longing for him.

Sketching a shrug, she said, 'I'll do whatever I think is best for me.'

With unforgivable frankness he said, 'You seem to make a habit of gathering up legacies. You started your business with the money one lover left you; were you Jacob Ward's lover too?'

For a moment Morna wasn't sure she'd heard him correctly. One glance at his unyielding face disabused her of that idea. In a voice so cold it should have frozen him off, she said distinctly, 'He was an old man.'

He said brutally, 'So?'

'So I don't have lovers old enough to be my grandfather.' She swung on her heel and walked away from him towards the bach, so filled with angry disgust she could barely see.

Clearly he agreed with the majority opinion, that she was a woman on the make. The thought stabbed her as she heard the sound of his car's engine die away up the hill.

Whipping up seething antagonism to cover the pain, she changed into a pair of jeans and a T-shirt and went for a long, brisk walk along the beach, ending up by climbing the hill behind the bach—land owned by Hawke—in a mood of furious defiance. There she watched the sun go down over Auckland in swathes of gold and garnet-red.

Grimly, as the colours leached away, fading so that the sky changed into an upturned bowl the shimmering lavender-pink of a kunzite crystal, she walked back home. It hurt to accept that what scored her heart was not so much anger as the sting of betrayal, but she faced that unpalatable fact without flinching.

Hawke was a hypocrite, kissing her like a lover and then accusing her of prostituting herself.

Although, to be fair, he'd kissed her *before* he'd found out that Jacob had left her the bach.

CHAPTER FIVE

'DON'T make excuses for him,' Morna told herself scornfully. She let herself into the bach and set about concocting some sort of dinner.

Clearly Hawke had heard gossip from someone at lunch, and was only too eager to believe it.

'So what's new about betrayal?' she asked aloud, looking with disfavour at the sandwich she'd slapped together.

All Hawke had done was kiss her. You couldn't count that fingertip on her throat—it didn't even register as a caress, because he'd been furious when he did it and he'd wanted to shame her.

She could cope with kisses and an insult. Especially as she wouldn't be seeing any more of him.

Cold with something too close to despair, she picked up the sandwich, trying hard to shut out the memory of her own shockingly uninhibited response whenever he'd touched her. It had given her more erotic pleasure than Glen's most inventive lovemaking.

Ferociously, Morna bit into the bread and began to chew, but with the sandwich only half eaten she sat down at her desk and began to play with designs.

Coral and pearls were traditional for a baby; if it was a girl, then perhaps a pearl a year? Clichéd, of course, but what woman wouldn't enjoy pearls? And with really good ones it could take decades to get a matched set...

She'd need to wait until Cathy's baby was born to see her colouring. Different pearls suited different skin tones.

And if it was a boy? She frowned. '*Not* a silver christening mug,' she said out loud.

With the uneaten sandwich beside her, she picked up the pencil and began sketching ideas. Planning for the baby eased a tender patch in her heart. It didn't seem likely now that she'd have children of her own, but she'd be an aunt to Nick and Cathy's offspring—the only one they'd have.

On Monday the dithering engaged couple arrived late for their interview, and took up precious time by embarking on a full-scale argument in front of her. Furious, Morna toyed with the idea of telling them to go elsewhere, but instead set herself to placating both of them and finding out what they really wanted.

Just after lunch something went wrong with the security system, locking two people in the shop until the expert on call arrived to let them out and reset the alarm. And after that she cut her forefinger. Small cuts were as normal as the grime left on her hands by jeweller's rouge, but this one bled enough for her to stick a plaster on it—not the look she wanted for an evening viewing of paua pearls at Auckland's ritziest hotel!

And she'd forgotten to find out how much she'd have to pay for rates for the Bay.

'Forget about it,' she said, creaming off the day's make-up and carefully reapplying more before donning the sleeveless top and skirt she'd packed that morning.

In the workroom she opened the safe and slipped one of her rings onto her finger; a shimmering Argyle diamond several shades lighter than her eyes, it glowed like a distant sun against her skin.

Annie, her assistant, came in. 'Don't you look the cool dude!' she said admiringly. 'Gosh, the safe's full.'

'Diamonds for that blasted engaged pair to choose from,' Morna told her, 'and some rubies. I finished the diamond necklace on Sunday; the owner's out of the country for a week or so, so it'll be there until she comes back. Oh, and Babs Pickersgill's pearls to restring, and a couple of other repairs which I'll do tomorrow.'

Babs's pearls were famous—a superb triple string of Broome blues inherited from her mother, exquisite and horrendously valuable. It was unfortunate that they didn't suit her skin colour.

The doorbell pealed imperatively. 'Sounds like a customer who knows what they want,' Annie said. 'Have fun!'

Annie was someone else who thought that Morna should have a social life.

In the hotel foyer, people were gathering to go out, chatting in a variety of languages and accents. Suddenly—and stupidly—aching with loneliness, Morna got into the lift. Outside the suite she showed her invitation to a couple of burly security staff before being ushered inside.

'Champagne, madam?' A waiter offered a tray of glasses, each filled with pale rosy-gold liquid.

Morna took one and looked around, noting the eclectic mix of people—as well as professionals in the field, the organisers of the show had asked enough of Auckland's glitterati to make sure the event got into the newspapers. She smiled and nodded at a couple of competitors, smiled more widely at a beaming Babs Pickersgill on the other side of the room, then waved to a friend.

The loneliness that had ambushed her in the hotel lobby returned; the glitter of the diamond on her finger seemed bleakly intrusive, an icy reminder that she was alone, that no man had ever cared enough for her to make a pledge of affection.

Grow up, she commanded; you don't trust any man enough to accept that sort of commitment. Or want it. Yet for a moment Hawke's strong, dominant face flashed across her mind's eye. When he made a threat, she thought, he meant it, and she suspected that he carried it out.

Would he be the same with a promise?

Glass in hand, she walked over to examine the pearls, gleaming hemispheres in shades of blue and green, displayed skilfully on sweeps of cream satin to emphasise their lustrous golden sheen. Excitement wiped away her tiredness and her worry, and her fingers tingled. What beauty she could create with these glorious things...

A buzz of chatter behind her finally permeated her concentration. Angling slightly, she sent a sideways glance towards the door.

And froze. Hawke had just walked in, and he'd seen her; her eyes were trapped by the narrowed jade brilliance of his. Unbidden, an incandescent delight soared through her.

Until she noticed the woman beside him.

Mouth stinging with remembered kisses, Morna stiffened her buckling knees and turned away, all the heat and fire drowned by one glimpse of long female fingers on Hawke's black sleeve. He was in a dinner jacket, which meant dinner later in the evening—and then what? Scorching images of him with the woman blotted the pearls from her sight.

What the hell was he doing here? She swallowed some champagne without tasting it as a hideous suggestion blazoned itself across her brain. Perhaps he'd deliberately come—perhaps he wanted to let her know that in spite of those kisses he was a free agent.

'Point taken,' she muttered beneath her breath, and took

another substantial sip of wine. When it hit her stomach she blinked and put the glass down.

Not that she could blame her dizziness on two mouthfuls of wine. Somehow seeing Hawke produced the same feeling she had when she came up with a design that suited a client while displaying the gems to their best advantage—the whole jewel harmonious and beautiful and strong.

Physically, he possessed the same intrinsic balance. Black hair and bronzed skin set off the pale clarity of his green eyes, and his outrageous good looks were based on a strong, harmonious framework. Combined with his height and athletic build, and a lethal grace that was all elementary male, he pleasured the eye.

Yet she'd seen handsome men before and felt nothing like this. With a bitter taste in her mouth, she accepted that even when she was furious with him she respected his formidable, uncompromising character. He was, if anything, too confrontational, but he hadn't lied to her.

The pearls swam before her eyes in a glimmer of sea-coloured iridescence. Pulses quivering, Morna tried to focus on them, so pathetically grateful when her friend came up that she hurried into speech.

'Fantastic, aren't they?' she said with a vague gesture at the cases, endeavouring to sound like a normal person instead of someone so keenly aware of one man that her skin registered his presence.

'Gorgeous.' Her friend, the manager of a large jewellery salon in the heart of the city, looked at her quizzically. 'I'll bet your creative juices are working overtime. How are things?'

'Fine, fine.' But Morna's attention wasn't on her friend, or even the luminous sea-coloured pearls. The woman on Hawke's arm had just flung her arms around him and kissed him. No air kiss, either—this was the real thing, although it didn't last long.

Snatching her gaze away, Morna concentrated on chatting, smiled, exchanged a bit of gossip, agreed to lunch the next week, and the moment the other woman had rejoined her husband couldn't remember a word they'd said. At least she'd got herself together enough to put the luncheon date in her diary, she thought with a slash of self-contempt.

Then Babs Pickersgill came up to greet her effusively. Kind, charity queen and a generous gossip, she said, 'Morna, you're the only person I trust to tell me—should I buy some of these? They are truly fabulous, but are they going to be a real investment?'

Morna took a deep breath. 'I think so. Although yours are—'

Babs gave a fleeting grimace. 'You know, I never think of them as mine—even though she's been dead for too many years, they're still my mother's!'

Her expression altered, melting into open eagerness as she looked over Morna's shoulder. 'Hawke,' she murmured in a stunned tone that was a tribute to his powerful male beauty.

He switched his unreadable gaze from Morna's face to Babs's, and said her name in a deep, amused voice that had the older woman preening.

Released from the searchlight intensity of her own reaction, Morna swallowed, desperate to escape.

Hawke noticed the shock in her whisky-gold eyes, the colour ebbing from her skin to reveal a subtle flick of blusher along her cheekbones. A primeval desire to hunt flamed into life; she was prey worth chasing down, he thought cynically.

But perhaps he was the prey.

Babs looked from his face to Morna's stony one, and gave a little laugh. 'Morna, this is—'

'Morna and I have already met,' Hawke told her politely, 'and I won't interrupt you. But later, Morna, may I bring someone across to talk to you?'

He sensed her reluctance, although nothing of it showed in her face. 'Yes, of course.'

'Thank you.'

When he stepped back Morna turned gratefully to her companion, who was craning to see where he went.

'Oh, yes, he *is* with Peri Carrington.' She looked from beneath her lashes at Morna. 'I've been hearing that things are really hotting up there—perhaps he's finally fallen in love! We never thought it would happen—he's been chased unmercifully since before he left school, poor boy, so it's no wonder he's completely cynical. But perhaps all he needed was a sweet, innocent girl.' She beamed.

'Quite possibly,' Morna said inanely.

'She's such a charming girl. Sir Philip's daughter—do you know the family?'

Sir Philip Carrington—oh yes, she knew him. And his mistress. But not his wife. 'I know of him,' Morna said quietly, and began to discuss pearls once more.

Ten minutes later she was alone again. A glance across the busy room revealed Hawke smiling down at another flirtatious woman while Peri Carrington clung to his arm. A pang of potent desire tore through Morna, mingled with that melancholy ache of longing.

Suddenly tired of the mingled aroma of perfume and wine, the subdued hum of conversation and air-conditioning, the busyness of the rapidly thickening crowd, she scanned the gems one last time before cutting through the crowd towards Hawke and the woman he was escorting. She wasn't going to wait for them to come to her; she'd conduct this interview on her own terms and in her own time.

Hawke must have had the same idea, because he turned, the woman still attached like a limpet to his arm.

Heart jumping nervously, Morna firmed her mouth in a brief, businesslike smile.

With an answering grin Hawke introduced Peri Carrington in a pleasant, neutral voice before finishing, 'Peri's looking for someone to design a ring for her.'

Murmuring conventional greetings, the two women shook hands. Peri said graciously, 'Hawke tells me you have great talent.'

'He's too kind,' Morna said just as graciously. What sort of ring?

Peri asked, 'Is that one of your own designs you're wearing?'

She couldn't have been more than twenty-two or three, and she wore her elegant dress with panache and an instinctive flair. Of course she was beautiful.

'Yes,' Morna said.

'It's lovely,' Peri said, her eyes on the ring. 'May I have a closer look?'

Morna stripped it from her finger and handed it over. It had been commissioned by a woman who'd decided she didn't want it, and although a little showy for Morna's taste, on the right hand it wasn't too ostentatious. Art Deco in style, the square golden diamond was flanked by princess-cut blue-white diamonds.

'It's—fantastic,' Peri breathed, sounding much younger than her years. 'May I try it on?'

'Do.'

Peri slid the ring onto her engagement finger and held her hand out, admiring it before sending a sultry glance up at Hawke. 'What do you think?'

His expression didn't change. 'Exquisite,' he said. 'Magnificent stones, and the craftsmanship is excellent. A very sophisticated product.'

Morna kept her eyes lowered, but a note in his voice chased a shiver the length of her spine. Ostensibly he was talking about the ring, but that last remark had been directed at its maker—and it was no compliment.

Peri laughed. 'Only you would call a fabulous thing like this a product,' she teased, and handed the ring back. 'Thank you very much. I'll call in one day and we can talk about things.'

'I'll look forward to that,' Morna said politely, and fished a business card from her bag. 'It will save you looking up the number.' She smiled at them both. 'I'm afraid I have to go,' she said, almost meeting Hawke's eyes.

'Another appointment?' His tone was cool and unemotional, the words just too swift to be drawled.

She gave him a meaningless smile. 'Yes,' she said evenly. 'Goodbye.'

Well, she did have another appointment—with her bed! But it had been unworthy as well as foolish to lie to him.

Outside it was fresh, but still warm for autumn; soon winter would arrive with its rain and chilly nights.

Hawke's voice echoed in her ears. *Inevitable as winter,* he'd said. Morna's throat closed up, but she shook her head angrily. No. *Never.* She didn't dare—making love with Hawke, even if he wasn't planning on marrying his charming young friend, would mark her for life.

When the valet brought her car around she got into it gratefully, senses humming and emotions chaotically fractured.

'I am not jealous,' Morna told herself between clenched teeth, negotiating narrow streets behind the hotel.

But she ached with it—burned with it—a pain so intense she actually felt it in every cell. Mortified, she concentrated on getting home safely.

Once there she had to force herself to eat a carton of yoghurt and drink some hot chocolate before going to bed.

Yet sleep eluded her for hours, her restless mind dwelling on scorching images of Hawke and the youthful Peri making wild, abandoned love in some great bed not too far away.

'Get out of my head,' she gritted, pummelling her pillow into submission. Why shouldn't he make love to anyone he wanted? Peri at least was younger than him, not a couple of years older!

Eventually she slept—so heavily that the telephone had been ringing in her dreams for some time before she managed to wake up enough to realise what was happening and fumble the handset close to her ear.

'Hello,' she groaned into it.

'Ms Vause?' Male, very official. 'Are you the owner of Vause's in Forsythe Street?'

Struggling to clear her brain of fog, she mumbled, 'Yes. Who is this?'

'The police, Ms Vause. I'm afraid your store has been ram-raided.' He paused, before adding flatly, 'Almost everything has been cleared out, including the contents of the safe—which does not appear to have been locked.'

Ten minutes later Morna was driving as fast as she dared up the hill, concentrating fiercely on keeping the car on the road. A full moon shone from both the sky and the sea, illuminating the fenceposts flashing by; when the surface changed to tarseal she eased her foot down further on the accelerator.

Just past the resort she took the blind corner at the top of the hill too quickly, and headed straight into the bril-

liance of headlights on full beam. Instinctively she hit the
brake and twisted the steering wheel away from the on-
coming vehicle. Her car skidded, bucking in the loose
gravel until finally it was halted abruptly by something
solid.

Flung against the seat belt in a cacophony of metallic
shrieks and groans, she gasped for breath and levered herself back against the seat. A dim memory made her release
her death grip on the wheel and grope blindly for the key.
Once she'd turned off the engine she could hear the other
vehicle, now stationary in the middle of the road with
lights dipped but the engine still running. Dazed, she
found the clip to her seat belt and had just released it
when the door was wrenched open.

'Are you all right?' a hard male voice demanded rapidly.

She blinked as the man crouched down beside the car.
Hawke.

'Yes,' she whispered, shrivelling in dismay.

In a voice she didn't recognise he asked, 'Nothing broken or hurting?'

She tried a tentative, experimental wriggle. 'My shoulder's bit sore, that's all.'

Of course he didn't take her word for it. 'Breathe in
deeply.'

She did.

'No pain?' This time his tone was steady and purpose-
ful.

'Not a bit.'

'Your ribs are all right, then. Try moving every muscle
in your body.'

That took a little longer, until eventually she said,
'They're all fine. Thank God for seat belts.' But her voice

trembled and she was seized by a sudden shameful need to bury her head in her hands and bawl.

'Indeed,' Hawke said curtly, standing up and stepping back. 'OK, see if you can get out.'

She began to ease herself up from the seat, but when her legs collapsed beneath her she wailed in horrified frustration, 'What's the matter with me? I'm not hurt.'

'Shock,' he said succinctly. With wonderfully gentle strength he lifted her out of the car as though she was as light and small as Cathy, and asked, 'Still no pain?'

'None except in my shoulder, and even that's easing. You can put me down—I really am all right.'

He scrutinised her face, his own features sharply prominent. Although her heart was pumping violently she met his eyes with what she hoped was her normal steadiness. Without saying anything he lowered her to her feet, but kept his arms around her.

Just as well, because the blood drained from her brain and she had to cling to him as she began to shiver. Almost clenching her teeth, she muttered, 'Damn, damn, damn!'

'Shock's a strange thing,' he said grimly, locking her against the hard support of his body in a protective embrace.

Heat poured into her, although it didn't stop her teeth chattering. 'B-but I wasn't hurt!'

'That makes no difference. Hang onto me; if you can't make it to my car I'll carry you.' The words and the deep cadences of his voice soothed her.

Just for a moment, she thought dizzily, and relaxed into the security of his great strength and the power that radiated from him.

In a minute she'd stop clinging to him and stand up straight. She knew her blood was circulating—she could hear it drumming in her ears and feel her heart throbbing in her chest—but it wasn't helping her regain her balance.

She looked up into Hawke's hard face, a sculpture of angles and planes picked out by the white brilliance of the moon. Beneath his lashes his eyes gleamed, and to her astonishment his mouth had softened into something almost like tenderness.

Her knees buckling, she realised with appalled disbelief that she was responding to him with acute physical awareness. It had to be shock, she thought desperately, but the urgent hunger consuming her, all flame and dazzle and piercing desire, didn't feel like shock...

And then he saved her. 'What the hell were you doing driving in the middle of the night with no lights on?' he asked in a gritty, tight voice.

Catapulted into chilly reality, Morna twisted around and stared at her car, crumpled against one of the sturdy fenceposts. 'No lights?' she croaked, because although none showed now, surely she'd turned them on?

'None,' he told her, his voice gentling. 'You need to sit down. Let me take your weight—yes, that's it.'

And because she thought she might shiver herself into a shame-inducing faint, she meekly let him half carry her across the road.

But when he'd inserted her into the passenger seat of his car she took a deep breath and protested, 'I wouldn't have been able to see without lights.' A thought struck her. 'Perhaps they failed when I hit the post?'

'You could see because it's bright moonlight.' He stood up and looked down at her with cool remoteness, all signs of that fugitive tenderness—if it had ever existed—vanishing. 'Trust me, they weren't on.'

Morna put a shaky hand to her forehead and leaned

back. Closing her eyes, she retraced her mad scramble out of the bach and into the car.

She'd flung on jeans and a thin woollen jersey, slipped her feet into canvas shoes, and grabbed bag and keys as she'd dashed outside to the car. And she remembered muttering furiously when she'd fumbled the door open in the darkness, then stabbing the key around until she'd managed to insert it and turn on the engine.

But her mind remained frighteningly blank about lights.

'All right?' Hawke asked quietly.

'Yes.'

The soft *thunk* when he closed the car door made her start. Head swirling, her body jumping with excess adrenalin, she opened her lashes a fraction to watch him stride across the road and examine her car.

Big and vital and dangerous, she thought wearily. But competent—and strangely kind in an emergency. She shut her eyes again.

Where had he been until now?

Peri Carrington's face flashed up like a neon sign against Morna's closed eyelids. Her mouth turned down at the corners in a small, painful grimace that didn't come close to a smile. No prize for answering that question! Almost certainly he'd spent the previous hours in his girlfriend's bed.

Forget it, she advised herself feverishly, trying to ignore the talons of pain that raked her heart; she had more important things to worry about than Hawke's lovers.

Had Annie forgotten to secure the safe? If so, the insurance company would refuse to pay out on its contents, and she'd have to find money to reimburse the clients whose pieces were stolen. Which meant borrowing money from somewhere. The bank? A gnawing panic hollowed out her stomach; if she couldn't raise the cash she stood to lose everything she'd worked so hard to achieve.

It was a relief when Hawke got into the car again. Hurrying into speech, she said in a muted tone, 'I'm sorry. Of all the stupid things to do! I suppose the moon was so bright—and I was in a tearing hurry. Not that that's any excuse. At least I didn't hit you.'

In a voice that could have started another Ice Age he said, 'You could have killed yourself.'

For some reason—oh, because she was still in shock!—she regretted the gentleness he'd shown before. With as much spirit as she could summon, she returned, 'Hitting a post was hardly going to kill me.'

'At the speed you were going it could have.' He set the car in motion and began to turn it on the narrow road.

Morna asked abruptly, 'What are you doing?'

'I'm taking you to a doctor.'

CHAPTER SIX

MORNA flinched and turned her head, fixing her gaze on the bold, austere line of Hawke's profile against the white austerity of the moonlight. 'But I'm fine, really I am.' Once more she moved her shoulders against the seat and ran her hand down between her breasts and over to one hip. 'Not a twinge.'

He glanced over his shoulder and smoothly reversed the car. 'You've had a shock and you need to see someone. Where were you going in such a hurry?'

'My shop's been burgled,' she said bleakly. Saying it, actually hearing the words, flat and heavy against the quiet sound of the engine, made it real. And much worse.

The car now faced back the way he'd come, its engine purring quietly, but Hawke didn't immediately set it going. Instead he turned his head and looked at her. 'When did that happen?'

Tensely she willed him to start driving. 'The police rang me a few minutes ago. It was a ram-raid. They smashed though the window with a truck and snatched everything they could.'

Her heart jumped when he picked up her taut hands and held them in a warm grip. 'I'm sorry,' he said.

'I have to get there,' she said, pulses thudding so hard she could hear them above her breathing. Don't be nice to me, she pleaded silently. I can't cope with it.

As if he'd heard her he released her and put the car into gear. 'I'll take you down—after you've seen a doctor.'

'I don't know any—'

'I do.'

She fumed silently. 'But the police want me to give them an inventory of what's been taken. I can't ask—'

'You're not asking,' he cut in with a patience that really set fire to her temper. 'I'm offering.'

'Oh, was that an offer?' she said sweetly. 'Funny, but it sounded like a command. *Shut up and do as you're told, Morna.*' She dragged in a rapid breath and put a hand to her temple, where a small hammer was making itself felt. 'For your information, I can manage my life without your interference.'

They had reached the main highway. Hawke slowed, then turned south and put his foot on the accelerator. The big engine howled softly before settling down to a steady hum.

'So far tonight you don't seem to have made much of a fist of it,' he said on a caustic note.

The adrenalin drained from her system, leaching away most of her antagonism. 'Oh, go to hell,' she muttered, not so far beneath her breath that he couldn't hear. 'I hate being told I'm wrong—even when I am. *Usually* I can manage my life.'

'I'm sure you can, but for tonight let me take care of you.'

Almost the worst thing about this whole situation was the temptation to do just that. Perhaps she'd damaged her head in the accident; for eight years she'd forged her own path through life, protecting her precious self-respect by making sure she was dependent on no one. But here she was, feeling vaguely grateful for his consideration and the cool assurance with which he'd taken over.

Narrowly she watched him punch a number into a mobile telephone on the dash.

When a weary voice—female—answered he said with warm sympathy, 'Yes, Elaine, I know what time it is. Sorry. Can you do something for me?' Concisely, his eyes on the road ahead, he described what had happened.

'Better bring her into the surgery,' the doctor said, sounding much less tired.

'Thanks. I'll see you in ten minutes.' When he'd clicked off the telephone he gave Morna another swift, hard look before turning his attention back to the road. She folded her lips tightly and said nothing, but a wistful thought taunted her.

If Hawke ever used that tone of voice with her, would she be able to resist it?

She'd have to; she valued her independence far too highly to yield it to any man, however charismatic and occasionally kind.

At Orewa he turned off the highway into a suburban street with a smart medical centre on one corner. The doctor, a pleasant middle-aged woman, banished Hawke to the waiting room and checked Morna over with impersonal skill and searching, gentle hands.

'You're in surprisingly good shape,' she said eventually. 'You must have been sitting dead straight in the seat when you hit the post. Most people get some bruises.'

Morna said, 'I told Hawke I was all right.'

'I can see how much notice he took of that.'

'I'm sorry you had to get up in the middle of the night for nothing because he panicked.'

The doctor's brows shot up. 'Panicked? Hawke? I don't believe it.'

Morna laughed reluctantly. 'Well, no, he didn't panic. He was his usual uncompromising self, handing out decisions like some conquering monarch. Does he ever lose his cool?'

'I've never seen it happen. He has a strong sense of duty,' the doctor told her cheerfully. 'Losing his father when he was twelve just added more steel and toughness to an already decisive character. His mother was so desperately unhappy that Hawke had to grow up fast. He's carried big responsibilities from an early age.'

While the doctor washed her hands Morna absorbed this information. It explained quite a lot about Hawke—his effortless authority, and that formidable, high-handed decisiveness.

'You know him well,' she said.

'His mother is my second cousin.' The tap was turned off, and the GP continued into the silence, 'The really irritating thing about him is that he's usually right; you could have been concussed. And if there was any possibility of a broken rib I'd have needed to send you for an X-ray.'

Out in the waiting room Hawke turned swiftly from the window, keen eyes searching Morna's face.

'She's fine,' the doctor said.

'No sign of shock?' Hawke asked.

'Teaching me my job?' But she gave him an affectionate smile. 'No more than you'd expect after a crash, and considerably less than most.'

Morna said crisply, 'So going to Auckland won't hurt me.'

'Depends what you plan to do there,' the GP said, looking from Morna's face to Hawke's watchful countenance.

Quickly Morna explained.

'The best thing would be to head home to bed, but you should be all right,' the doctor told her. 'Just don't overtax yourself.'

After Morna had thanked the older woman, Hawke took her elbow and steered her out to the car. Being Hawke,

of course, he wasn't content to leave it. 'Are you sure you
need to go to town?' he asked. 'You heard what Elaine
said—you should be in bed.'

'You don't have to take me—I can get a taxi from
here.'

He delivered another razor-sharp glance and put the key
in the engine. 'Why can't it wait until morning?'

'Because it's my responsibility.'

And because she needed to see for herself that the safe
hadn't been secured. Nausea clutched her; as the car sped
down the road to Auckland she leaned her head back
against the seat and closed her eyes, totting up how much
the contents were worth. It was a calculation she'd already
made in her mad scramble to get dressed, and its answer,
she thought mordantly, spelt bankruptcy.

Moonlight flooded the silent road as they drove south.
Morna's head drooped, but dread and will-power kept her
eyes open.

Half an hour later she emerged from the back room, shivering in the cool night air and staring at the mess some
career criminal had made of her window using a thumping
great vehicle with bull bars. She said something brief and
explicit, and saw amusement in Hawke's face before he
looped an arm around her shoulders. Although she stood
stiffly beside him, the casually sympathetic action con-
jured warmth from deep inside her.

The young constable said, 'It was a quick, professional
job—in and out and long gone before your security firm
got here. Ms Vause, if it's not too much trouble, I'd like
you to come along to the station for a few minutes so we
can go over the inventory.'

'What's happening with the window?' Hawke asked.

'Security will deal with it,' Morna said tightly. Her

head was pounding and she was so cold she couldn't feel her toes. Although the night was chilly, the cold came from inside her. When she closed her eyes she could still see the safe, its door gaping open with no sign of forcing; Annie had forgotten to secure it, and the raiders had taken everything.

Hawke nodded. 'Come on, Morna—you can't do anything more here. I'll take you to the station.'

He admired her courage and her sturdy determination, but the sooner she got home the better. For a moment he toyed with the idea of taking her to a hotel after she'd given the police whatever they wanted. Her eyes were too big and smoky in her composed face, and every so often her husky voice quivered. She was maintaining a gallant façade, but only just—and she resented him seeing what she clearly saw as weakness.

Taking her arm, Hawke urged her out of the shop across the footpath, surprised when she made no objection. Beside the car he looked down at her face, pale in the unkind glare of a street lamp, and ruthlessly endured a surge of hunger, burning through him like a blast furnace. Did she know that the dark clothes and the tumble of sable hair gave her a decadent, seductive glamour?

Probably. The lady was well able to look after herself, so why not leave her to it?

Because his mother had brought him up to be protective, although she probably wouldn't be happy about him protecting this woman.

And because that quiver in her voice cut up his defences like a stealth bomber.

It could all be an act, of course. If gossip was to be believed, she knew exactly how to pander to the male ego.

Unfortunately, being half convinced that she was a mercenary opportunist didn't subdue the urgent desire claw-

ing at him. For an incredulous moment he even found
himself thinking that a deprived childhood might well
give rise to such an outlook.

Coldly angry with himself for being gullible, he said,
'Let's go, Morna.'

She sent him a tired glance and bent to open the car
door. 'Thank you,' she tossed over her shoulder before
sinking carefully into the passenger seat and folding in
her long, sexy legs.

A self-derisive smile quirked the corners of Hawke's
mouth in as he walked around to the driver's side and got
in. He pulled away from the kerb, wondering what was
going on behind her closed expression.

She was sitting erect, shoulders held stubbornly square,
her profile tight and remote against the lights outside.
Somehow she seemed smaller, her silky black hair in a
loose swathe across her shoulders, her dramatic features
pinched.

To Morna's relief the interview at the station took only
a few minutes. She explained how the security system
worked, gave the constable an inventory detailing the contents of the safe, and told him she'd contact the clients
whose jewellery had been in it.

When it was over he walked her to the office door; she
looked through it and saw Hawke talking to a tall man
who bore an air of authority.

Beside her, the constable said, 'And you trust your assistant?'

'Absolutely,' she stated with conviction. 'I'm certain
she had nothing to do with it.'

'We'll want to see her just the same,' he said noncom-
mittally.

Hawke looked across, reminding her of the way Nick

always seemed to know where Cathy was. Don't be stupid, she thought grimly.

Back in the car, she said in a low, awkward voice, 'Thank you for this.'

'Don't worry. I caught up with a friend I used to play rugby with when I was at university.'

She nodded. 'I saw you talking to someone.'

He glanced across and caught her eye. As he switched his gaze back to the road he noticed her moisten her lips.

In spite of everything she couldn't hide the fact that she wanted him. Heat kindled again in his loins and he wondered grimly if it was the edge of danger that he found so sexually exciting about her.

Her response to his kisses had been nothing short of explosive. So was yours, a cynical voice in his brain warned. Hawke liked women, he enjoyed everything about them, and although he wasn't promiscuous he was experienced.

Physically Morna was getting to him. No other woman had dented the cool control he valued so much; he'd never met one he wanted beyond reason. It was up to him to make sure he didn't let himself get entangled in the tawny fire of her eyes or seduced by exquisite skin and a body that was a sultry invitation.

And if he was to get them safely home he'd better ignore the sheer lust clamouring through his unruly body.

Morna stared through the window, eyelids drooping. Although exhaustion weighted her bones she didn't dare let herself relax enough to slip over the edge of sleep. Still, it was hypnotically peaceful to sit beside Hawke as the car hummed along empty streets towards the Harbour Bridge. Blinking at the street lamps, she let her brain slip into neutral.

Once they left the city the sparse traffic dwindled further, and soon the road stretched emptily ahead, snaking up hills and through valleys where no lights shone.

'All right?' Hawke's voice was cool and self-sufficient.

'Fine,' she replied automatically.

From the corner of her eye she watched his hands on the wheel—lean, long-fingered, steering with a confident economy of movement. A secret, warm reassurance seeped into her; a woman would be safe in those hands, she thought drowsily.

And stiffened with alarm as she sensed the trap opening at her feet. No man was safe; love made all of them dangerous. Even Nick had hurt Cathy...

'What made you decide to move into Jacob's bach?' Hawke asked.

Morna turned her head to survey a long, curved beach, gleaming spectrally under the moon. His question sounded like idle conversation, the sort of thing you might say to while away a long drive. Morna didn't make that mistake; as this was Hawke, of course it wasn't. 'I wanted some peace and quiet, and it's cheap.'

'And that's important?' His tone was almost uninterested.

She stiffened slightly, then relaxed. 'To anybody starting out in business on their own, yes.'

'I'm surprised Nick didn't suggest that you move in with him.'

'I love Nick devotedly,' she said with composure, 'but he's never got over being a big brother. I value my independence too much to move in with him and Cathy.'

'Will you get insurance for the contents of the safe?'

Keep calm, she told herself. Although he'd been there when she'd seen the empty safe, he had no idea what was in it. 'I don't know.'

'I don't suppose it matters too much.' He slipped the

car into another gear as they approached lights. 'With Nick's backing—'

'Nick doesn't back me. He never has. A business that relies on hand-outs from friends or family can hardly be called a business.' Deliberately offhand, she settled back into the seat and pretended to yawn. Her financial affairs were none of his concern. 'I wish I knew who'd done this.'

'So you could punish them?'

His perception scared her a little. Throat tightening, she said fiercely, 'It's like a violation.' And immediately wondered if he'd think she was a drama queen.

But he said quietly, 'I understand that.'

At her startled look he shrugged. 'It's something you've conceived and created, a part of you. Naturally any attack on it is personal.'

He did understand. Morna was turning this over in her mind when he asked, 'What made you decide that designing and making jewellery was your dream?'

'It seemed a logical progression. Nick always thought I had talent, and so did...' Her voice trailed away.

Although Glen had professed to admire her creativity, he'd put a stop to her ambition to study design because he'd wanted all of her attention. His cynical kiss-off still stung; pride had demanded she fling his bribe in his face, but if she'd done that Nick would have insisted on supporting her. And she'd needed desperately to get away from the naked humiliation of being thrown out like yesterday's garbage. So she'd accepted, and spoiled Glen's gesture by paying him back.

'You and Nick grew up together?'

In spite of Hawke's casual tone she knew he'd have picked up what she'd almost said. It didn't matter; he must know she'd been Glen's mistress. Yet she felt smirched.

She sat up straighter and said crisply, 'He joined our family when he was seven, but before that he lived next door for as long as I can remember.'

Hawke didn't ask about the circumstances of Nick's arrival in the house she and her mother had shared with the occasional transient man, and she had no intention of telling him. He'd been born to wealth and privilege, not in a rundown, hopeless suburb, where the only people with a purpose had been the drug dealers.

'So how did you go about being a jewellery designer as opposed to a jewellery maker?' Hawke asked.

She shrugged. 'I studied hard and passed all my exams.' Her tone was perfectly steady.

A nicely sanitised version of the facts, Hawke thought sardonically. His swift sideways glance took in her tension; her hands were folded neatly in her lap, the long legs taut. He looked ahead again, trying to banish the memory of her spread out on the lounger at the Hardings' lunch party—silken skin softly gilded by the sun, narrow waist and broad shoulders setting off breasts that sent a grinding need prowling through him.

Irritated to find himself admiring her tenacity and her talent, as well as the hard work it had taken to turn herself into a success, he reminded himself that she'd used that seductive body as start-up capital.

For some ridiculous reason the idea of her as another man's lover ate into Hawke's gut. He refused to admit to jealousy, but this was a close cousin.

She was certainly an interesting mix of contradictions. Something in her voice had rung completely true when she'd stated that she refused to allow Nick to support her. Hawke wondered what it would be like to lay siege to such fierce independence...

Pretending to doze, Morna closed her eyes, eventually

slipping into a light, restless sleep. When the car stopped she woke with a start, unhappy fragments of dreams still chasing through her brain so that she said stupidly, 'What—where are we?'

'At the gate to the resort.' Hawke's voice was harsh.

Her lashes stuck together, but she forced them up. 'Why have we stopped here?'

'Because you have to make a decision.'

'What?'

The lamps at the entrance gleamed on his hard face, transforming the angles and planes into a bronze mask— beautiful, inflexible. 'Either you come in and spend the rest of the night here, or I take you back to the bach and stay with you.'

'No!' she said, heart jumping.

'One or the other.'

Her eyes dilated as he reached out and touched the damp track of a tear beneath one with a surprisingly gentle finger. 'You're in no fit state to be by yourself,' he said, as though explaining a simple fact. 'I imagine the shock of totalling your car and dealing with the burglary is finally making itself felt. So which is it to be?'

'The bach,' she said instantly. Once they got there she could get rid of him.

He smiled ironically and set the vehicle in motion again, leaving her distinctly uneasy.

But his ultimatum had made her remember something. 'I shouldn't just abandon my car on top of the hill,' she said fretfully. 'It might be dangerous to any other motorist.'

'It's not there.' When her head whipped around he said, 'While you were in the surgery I called the local tow-truck operator and got him to collect it.'

Morna sucked in a deep breath and said with rigid precision, 'I haven't thanked you for everything you've done tonight.'

'You did, and you don't need to.'

Was that a note of irony in his voice? She flashed a suspicious look at him, but his beautiful mouth was held severely in check.

It was cold when she got out of the car at the bach, and she stumbled, clutching for the door handle. Although she missed it Hawke had already caught her arm. He held her until she recovered her balance.

'All right?' he asked harshly.

'I'm fine,' she said, infusing her words with as much brisk confidence as she could summon. 'I was just a bit stiff.'

'Are you in pain? Bruised?' The questions came out like bullets.

'Not at all—not even a twinge!' She strode off across the grass, acutely aware of him walking with her so silently she couldn't hear a sound above the soft hush of wavelets on the beach and the dim thunder of her own heart. The air smelt fresh and grassy, and a soft easing of the darkness in the east meant that dawn wasn't too far away.

At the back door she turned and smiled up at him. 'Really, Hawke, you don't need to stay the night—there's only an hour or so of it left!'

'Nevertheless, I'm going to.'

She grabbed for her composure. 'I'll ring you tomorrow morning. In fact, I'll make use of the hotel shuttle to get into Orewa, if that's all right—I need to hire a car.'

'I'm staying, Morna.'

'Well, you can't, I'm afraid,' she said, carefully concealing any hint of satisfaction in her tone. 'There's only one bed.'

'I hope it's a big one,' he said laconically, taking the key from her suddenly nerveless grip and unlocking the bach door. He pushed it open, and to Morna's astonishment walked in ahead of her.

Chilled, she realised that he was checking the bach with an automatic caution. After a silent moment he found the light switch and turned it on.

'You're shivering,' he said. 'Get inside quickly.'

Instead she stood her ground and said grimly, 'I don't know what makes you think you're entitled to sleep with me for helping me, but if it's so important to you send me a bill, and when I pay it you can spend the money on a prostitute. That way we'll be square.'

His eyes glittered with splinters of ice. 'What a commonplace mind you've got,' he said in a pleasant tone that sliced her composure into shreds. 'I said you had a choice. Perhaps I should have told you that there are two bedrooms in my house at the resort. But you're not going to spend the night alone—look at you! You're barely able to stand up straight. Shock does odd things to the human system.'

She forced words out between gritted teeth. 'I must have told you three times tonight that I don't need a keeper or a nursemaid!'

He sent her a hooded, dangerous look. 'I disagree.'

For a moment she thought she was going to lose control completely, but she fought back her anger enough to say with harsh distinctness, 'Just go home.'

Silence drummed between them, charged with unspoken, unbearable emotions, until Hawke said implacably, 'Make up your mind. I stay here, or you come back to the resort with me.'

'I refuse to be whispered about as your latest lover.'

And then she remembered. 'What about—Peri? Wasn't that her name? The woman with you earlier tonight?'

His lashes drooped. 'What about her?'

Only that he might have made love to her before coming back to the resort! 'I don't imagine she'd be pleased if you spend what's left of the night with another woman,' Morna pointed out, seething at the involuntary wobble in her voice.

'How will she know? Do you plan to tell her?'

Morna pushed a weary hand across stinging eyes and snarled, 'You're being deliberately obtuse. Of course I won't tell her. But if I stay in your house everyone at the resort will be gossiping about it before either of us wake up in the morning. You know what small communities are like! And from then it will only take five minutes to reach Auckland!'

'I don't care,' he said ruthlessly, 'and I have to admit to some surprise at the prospect of it worrying you.'

Morna tried to whip up indignation, but an exhausting heaviness was weighing down both her body and her mind. She could only say, 'Not everybody can afford such a lofty disregard of other people's opinions.'

His broad shoulders lifted in a shrug. 'I don't think you give a damn. Come on, make up your mind, Morna. Now.'

Wavering, she bit her lip before glancing at his formidable face. He looked capable of staying there for what remained of the night, no matter how uncomfortable it was. Clamping her hand over a huge yawn, she finally muttered, 'As the alternative is making you spend the night in a chair here, I suppose I owe it to you to go back to the resort.'

CHAPTER SEVEN

IF HAWKE had shown any triumph Morna would have reneged on her admission of defeat, but he must have realised that because his expression didn't alter.

He said, 'You don't owe me anything. Do you want to collect some clothes?'

With a quick, furious nod she finally strode into the bach, walking past him as though he wasn't there. In the bedroom she scooped up a long T-shirt and the first clothes she came to, stuffing them into an elderly pack before collecting toiletries.

On the way out she pulled a face at her reflection in the speckled mirror. Although she hadn't injured herself in the car crash she looked more than weird—colourless as milk, with huge dark eyes and a mouth that trembled in the weak glare of the single lightbulb!

She switched off the light and walked into the bach's living room. Without haste Hawke looked up from the table. He'd been checking out her designs, she realised, no doubt after looking around the small room with patrician astonishment. Perhaps he'd never been in such seedy surroundings before!

Refusing to be ashamed of it, she announced, 'I'm ready,' each word a challenge.

'These are brilliant,' he said quietly.

It was stupid to feel so...so *exalted* by his praise, yet she couldn't hide the flush of involuntary pleasure. 'Thank you,' she said, with as much composure as she could manage.

Hawke's house was a complete contrast to the bach's shabby informality. A few steps from the beach, it faced the sun and nestled into a big fenced garden where banana palms waved great elephant-ear leaves only slightly shredded by the wind.

Furnished by the same decorator who'd made such a success of the resort, the interior of the house breathed calm good taste that soothed the tension knotting her stomach. Waves of exhaustion dragging her under, Morna clenched her jaw on a yawn as she followed Hawke into a wide hall.

'This is the spare bedroom,' he said, opening the door into a room decorated in peaceful shades of sand and cream and driftwood.

'It's already made up,' he said when he saw her staring at the queen-sized bed that dominated the room.

Ready for action, she thought, but the caustic retort remained unspoken when he added in a voice that came close to gentleness, 'Sleep well, Morna. If you need anything, let me know.'

After watching the door close behind him she stirred herself enough to wash her face in the small *en suite* bathroom before stripping off her clothes to crawl into a long T-shirt. Five minutes after she'd pulled the bedclothes up, sleep enveloped her in mindless darkness.

Until dreams began to wind through the darkness, jumbling images and emotion in an incoherent flood so painful she couldn't bear them. Still locked in restless slumber, she searched desperately in the clouded reaches of her mind for some refuge.

And then warmth enfolded her—warmth and unlimited security backed by a faint, tantalising scent she knew she'd recognise if only she weren't trapped in this web of despair. Salty, indefinably male, it was familiar yet foreign, and she liked it...

'Wake up,' a deep voice said quietly. A hand stroked the tangled hair from her face, smoothing it back in a sensuous caress. 'Wake up, Morna. It's only a nightmare, just a tangle of memories and old, tattered emotions. You can deal with it.'

She muttered, 'Hawke?' and the last baleful images collapsed into nothingness, vanquished by the solid comfort of his lean, superbly fit body.

'Yes.'

Forcing her eyes open, she blinked back tears. Hawke was sitting on the side of the bed with her in his arms. Although she could barely see his face, the grey light seeping through the curtains told her it was already day.

'Oh, rats!' she said hoarsely.

His chest lifted and she realised he was laughing. But his hand still stroked her hair from her damp face.

'Crying over your dreams doesn't go with your image,' he agreed, amusement threading his tone. 'It's all right. I won't tell anyone that you wake up looking like a houri, all smoky eyes and skin like crumpled silk, and red inviting lips...'

Dark lashes almost covering his eyes, he touched the corner of her mouth with the knuckle of his forefinger. 'That's a very erotic little crease right there,' he said, a raw note driving the humour from his voice.

Morna stared into eyes shimmering like molten jade. He was naked from the waist up, and the heat of his bronzed skin roused a latent tigress inside her. The silence in the room became a presence, thrumming with forbidden temptations, dangerous challenges. She wanted to turn and press her mouth to the long, sleek muscles in his shoulders, tantalise the gleaming, tanned skin with tiny bites and then stretch out with him...

The only thing saving her was the force of that flood of erotic fervour; it drained her of the strength she'd need to pursue such a forbidden desire.

Instead she shoved the heels of her hands to her eyes, trying to shut out every sensation and only succeeding in intensifying them. As she drank in the subtle, stimulating scent of his skin she thought dimly that it was no wonder he'd banished the dream. The all-pervading despair had had no chance against the craving that ate through her defences.

How could she be so susceptible to a man she didn't like, much less trust? Being with him sharpened her senses and set her alight. And when she was alone she missed his presence with a bone-deep longing, as though his absence drained her life of flavour and light.

He was a stud, she thought bleakly. Scratch that polished sophistication and you found an alpha male, tough and ruthless, his coldly intelligent mind and emotions leashed by will-power and discipline.

Totally unlike Glen, who'd demanded constant adoration to stoke his ego. And if she let herself be snared by this enervating, potent attraction for Hawke she'd end up regretting it even more than she regretted the waste of loving Glen.

Awkwardly she scrambled free of Hawke's embrace, yanking down the T-shirt as she shot across the bed and clambered off, to stand a pace away and fix him with an accusing glare.

He didn't try to hold her, but he didn't get up either. Insultingly confident, clad only—and heart-shakingly—in pyjama trousers several shades darker than his eyes, he couldn't have made it more plain that a woman's bed, a woman's sleep-warmed body, was nothing new to him.

Pretending a poise she didn't feel, she said stiffly, 'I'm sorry I woke you.'

'What was it all about?' Although his words were of ordinary, conventional concern, his voice hinted at a raw awareness, exciting and intensely unsafe.

Morna clenched the fingers that longed to run through the light scroll of hair across his chest. 'I can't remember,' she said, her mouth dry as her body responded with indecent eagerness to his untrammelled maleness.

'It happens that way with nightmares,' he said, and got to his feet.

Morna's poise shattered into splinters of ridiculous apprehension. She said quickly, 'Thank you for—for waking me out of it.'

His sensual mouth curved, and his eyes drifted from her mouth to her throat. 'It would always be a pleasure to wake you,' he said gravely.

Heat burned through Morna's skin. Beneath the mocking politeness of his tone a rasping note fixed her tumbling brain onto thoughts of powerful male desire, of timeless pleasure spent locked together in a mindless, animal mating...

Sweet, wild temptation, she thought dazedly, listening to the erratic jerk of her heartbeat as her body softened into a rich, passionately female expectancy.

She wanted him to wake her up in a thousand inventive ways—all of them involving arousal and eventual fulfilment. She wanted to wake him, and sate herself in the erotic promise he exuded from every sleek inch of his bronzed skin.

A shocking desperation frazzled her nerve-endings, deluging the pitiful remnants of her common sense with rea-

sons for walking into his arms and yielding to the driving
pulse of hunger that racked her body.

She had better get the hell out of here.

'I need to go home,' she said, the words tumbling over
each other. After a deep breath and some forceful com-
mands to her flagging will-power, she began again. 'It's
still quite early, isn't it? I'll walk.'

'And set every tongue in the resort wagging at top
speed?' he said sardonically. 'Last night you didn't want
that. Get dressed. Breakfast's on its way.'

'I don't—'

The words dried on her tongue as he pulled her into
his arms, tightening them behind her in slow, deliberate
torment. Glints of fire lit his eyes. So close now, she could
see that other colours varied the jade: sprinkles of gold
and a darker green—even a few shimmering streaks of
blue.

Elemental, white-hot sensation arrowed to the most responsive parts of her body.

Eyes glinting below half-closed lashes, he surveyed her
face with thorough consideration. 'You owe me an apology.'

'I do not!' But her tone didn't convey the indignation
and scorn that surely lurked beneath the pulsing anticipation. Instead she sounded hesitant and husky and dazzled. 'Last night you said I owed you nothing.'

'I changed my mind. Accusing me of expecting you to
sleep with me was a low blow.'

'I know,' she said, flushing as she remembered. 'I'm
sorry.'

'I don't think that's apology enough.' He showed his
teeth in a smile that hinted of wolf. 'I was hurt.'

'Hurt! You—?'

Hawke lowered his head and the heat she needed

swamped her in fire. Morna closed her eyes in silent surrender, only to have them fly open again when his warm, sneaky mouth came to rest on the corner of one brow.

He kissed the breadth of her cheekbone and bit the lobe of her ear. When she jumped and strangled a whimper in her throat he laughed softly and bit the sensitive lobe again, a little harder this time.

How could she burn and shiver at the same time? She shaped his name, but no sound emerged. Her heart thudded in her ears, and she flinched as his lips discovered the leaping pulse at the base of her throat.

Just below her ear was a tiny spot she'd never known about; when Hawke kissed her there she gasped, because lightning raced to her breasts and the pit of her stomach, inflaming the aching, clamorous place inside her that hungered for this man.

His lips traced a leisurely, erotic path down her throat, while one hand slid to cover a soft breast, knowledgeable fingers cupping it for a heated second before finding the shameless tip.

His head came up and he laughed in his throat, holding Morna's eyes with a smouldering, intent gaze. 'You excite me,' he said quietly, and finally kissed her properly, his mouth hard and fierce and carnal.

As hard and fierce and carnal as his body, she thought, her own responding with a storming violence that should have terrified her. It didn't; she gloried in the friction as they strained together, in the strength of the arms tightening around her and the blatant pressure against her, in the blunt, no-holds-barred demand of his mouth as he plundered hers.

Nothing—nobody!—had ever exerted this power over her; she was ravished by desire, aching with it, made wanton by it.

And then he raised his head and looked down into her face, and said in a voice in which irony and self-derision were mingled, 'So much for trying to make your spending the night here appear a perfectly normal situation. Anyone who sees your face and your mouth is going to know exactly what we've been doing.'

Morna dragged air into her famished lungs. If he could switch from passion to irony in an instant, so could she, because she didn't dare let him see how much he affected her.

But first she had to get out of his arms.

She lowered her own, which had somehow crept up to encircle his neck, and pulled away. Outraged, her body punished her by locking each muscle, but when Hawke released her she managed to take a couple of steps backward. Although it drained every remaining ounce of strength, she forced herself to stand upright and look at him, big and golden and overwhelming in the rapidly lightening room. She even coaxed a smile to the lips that had surrendered so abjectly.

'I think it was a losing battle,' she said wryly.

Her voice surprised her. Oh, tension sharpened it, and beneath that lingered a residue of hunger, but she didn't sound like a woman who'd just thoroughly and humiliatingly lost it in his arms.

Or discovered something she'd never thought existed... And that thought scared her even more than his effect on her.

Hawke said calmly, 'After we've had breakfast I'll take you home.'

Bitterly Morna realised that those moments of passion hadn't been a time of discovery for him. He was completely in command of himself, handsome face coolly self-sufficient, voice objective, eyes amused.

Keep your cool, Morna told herself. Slowly she breathed in until her voice was steady. 'Thanks for the offer of breakfast, but I need to go home now.'

One black brow lifting, Hawke said blandly, 'In that case I'll drive you there,' and left the room.

Morna gathered the clothes she'd packed the previous night and hurried into the bathroom. She showered swiftly, ending with a disciplinary freezing deluge in an attempt to control her reckless body.

It didn't work, but when she'd cleaned her teeth and applied make-up with a practised hand it was the ordinary Morna who gazed from the mirror. Ordinary, that was, apart from her mouth. Its full contours suspiciously approached the lush, pouting look usually only made possible by collagen injections!

That was when she remembered the reason she was here, in Hawke's house. Last night ram-raiders had struck the shop, and she was probably headed on the path to bankruptcy. Yet, although panic pooled in a cold mass beneath her ribs, the memory of his arms, his kisses, still warmed her in an illusion of safety. She set her jaw and went back into the bedroom.

But once there she opened the curtains, dawdling for a cowardly few minutes to survey the courtyard outside.

Like the house, it had been organised with a skilfully creative hand. A swimming pool gleamed blue-green, and furniture in dark wood sheltered from the sun in the shade of the wide overhang from the roof. Against a wall a puka tree waved huge, glossily boat-shaped leaves at the end of its parasol of sinuous branches. Frilled, flamboyant hibiscus blooms mingled with the soothing blue of plumbago blossoms and the scented, fleshy flowers of a frangipani, and there were palms, casually tropical, clustered around a sheet of water that fell into the pool.

'Putting things off isn't going to make them go away,' she said in a brittle voice, and picked up her pack and left the room.

Following her ears, she arrived in the sitting room, where she admired the decorator's restraint in integrating modern furniture with several old pieces. No silk, she noticed, and no wickerwork; a man of Hawke's size and presence would overwhelm anything but solid furniture.

A door on the other side of the room opened as she started towards it, to reveal Hawke.

'How do you feel?' he asked, scrutinising her face.

Thankful to see him clad in long trousers and a well-cut cotton shirt with short sleeves, she averted her eyes from the coiled muscles in his arms and cursed the betraying splash of hot colour along her cheekbones.

'All right,' she said, wondering what he meant. Was he asking how his kisses had affected her? Turned her into an addict, she suspected...

'No bruises?'

'*Bruises?*' She stared at him.

His brows shot up. 'You hit a fencepost last night,' he reminded her mildly.

Oh, God, just another thing she'd forgotten completely.

So pull yourself together and remember, she ordered herself. Aloud she said, 'Last night. Yes, no bruises. I was lucky.'

'Very.' He looked at the pack she was carrying and came into the room. 'I'll take that.'

Nobody appeared to be about when Hawke drove through the resort. Neither of them spoke. Morna kept her eyes fixed on the filmy white trail an aircraft made across the sky on its way to the rest of the world. Then she examined the gardens, lush with more palms and riotous cascades of bougainvillaea in various incarnations of scarlet and mauve and magenta.

Neither vapour trail nor gardens drove out the memory of Hawke's mouth on hers, or calmed the intense turmoil churning around inside her.

In her experience men who went in for unselfish altruism were rare birds indeed; even Nick loved her because he'd grown up with her. She knew what Hawke wanted from her—sex—and for the first time ever she was extremely tempted.

Quite a few of her friends indulged in uncommitted sex and emerged unscathed. Why shouldn't she? Loving Glen had stripped her of her hard-won confidence and self-esteem, but without love there'd be no risk of that, and no pain.

And Hawke wasn't in love with her. Oh, he was surprisingly considerate, and last night he'd been more than kind when he wasn't ordering her about, but really all they shared was this ferocious, sizzling, edgy attraction—nothing emotional, no bonds, no loyalty.

An affair was the logical way to exorcise it.

But there was Peri Carrington.

Morna flexed her suddenly curled fingers. OK, before she even considered taking the next step into intimacy she'd have to find out what the younger woman meant to Hawke; she wanted him, but not enough to be a shameful secret while he courted someone else.

So how would she do that? A straight question would be too blatantly obvious...

Anyway, one kiss and some sparks didn't give her the right to quiz Hawke about his relationships. And perhaps it was the shock he'd been so concerned about that made her even think of letting down her barriers. Or a weak need for support?

She looked up as the car halted, startled to see that they'd reached the bach.

Hawke said, 'Don't worry about catching the shuttle; I'll take you into Orewa. When do you want to go?'

'Oh, no, it's all right,' she said automatically. When he turned a cool, mocking smile on her she blundered on, 'You must have other things to do.'

He got out and opened the back door, leaning in to remove her pack. 'It will be my pleasure,' he said with a sardonic edge to the words.

Morna made a point of climbing out of the car as gracefully as she could. Time to establish a modicum of dignity and authority, even though last night she'd chosen to pack—for some reason hidden in the sleep-deprived depths of her brain—trousers in a wild black and white zebra-skin print. At least she hadn't brought the shirt that went with them, although her slinky black silk T-shirt wasn't exactly dignified or authoritative.

With canvas shoes she must look a sight.

'You've done more than enough for me,' she said, hiding her awkwardness with a brisk tone.

'I need to go to my office in Orewa,' he told her coolly, 'so ferrying you there will be no problem. And when you get in touch with your insurance company give them my name as a reference.'

That cold feather of fear brushed over her. 'I'll see what they say,' she temporised, glad to reach the bach. After she'd unlocked it and pushed the door open she turned. 'Thanks for everything,' she said simply.

'Are you going to get in touch with Nick?' When she didn't answer he elaborated, 'Nick Harding.'

'I know who you meant.' She lowered her lashes against the keen intensity of his gaze. In a stiff voice she said, 'He and Cathy are overseas. Not that I'd contact him anyway; I don't run to him with every little problem.' She summoned a smile. 'Not now, anyway. He has a greater loyalty in his life, and that's the way it should be.'

His eyes narrowed. 'Loyalty is important to you?'

Her shoulders moved uneasily beneath the fine black silk. 'Isn't it to everyone?' she parried.

'I suppose it is.' After a rapid glance at his wristwatch, he said, 'I'll see you in an hour's time.' And left her with a smile that came uncomfortably close to being satirical.

Once alone, she felt deflated and somehow empty, as though Hawke had taken her energy with him. While she ate breakfast, drank a stiff cup of coffee and changed into her severest black business suit, Morna wondered at that smile.

She checked her lipstick and combed her hair back from her face. Yes, she looked businesslike, ready for anything. Just as well, because today was not going to be a good one. She had to ring the clients whose jewellery had been stolen from the safe—tell dear Babs Pickersgill that her mother's pearls were gone—and she had to deal with the insurance company, who had every right to refuse to pay out on the contents of the safe.

And if that happened she had to find the money to repay her clients.

CHAPTER EIGHT

HAWKE'S eyes narrowed when he arrived to pick her up. 'That outfit should keep the insurance assessor's mind well and truly off his work,' he said as the big car took the hill with insulting ease.

'What?'

His mouth hardened into a taunting line. 'Tight black suit, long black legs, high heels, red lipstick. Man bait.'

'Goodness,' she said on a low purring note, angry yet relishing the stimulation his presence roused, 'and here I was thinking I was formal and businesslike and sophisticated—just right for a day spent with carpenters and glaziers and insurance personnel. But then, I come from the wrong side of the tracks, so how would I know about the right clothes to wear? And perhaps I should point out to you that any of those carpenters, glaziers and insurance assessors could be female.'

To her frustration he laughed softly. 'I like your smart mouth. I'm sorry—that was crass.'

'Absolutely,' she said, a little mollified.

He asked idly, 'Who are you insured with?' When she told him he nodded. 'They're a good firm. Remember, if I can help with anything, tell me.'

'Thank you,' she said, made cautious by the warm glow his casual offer had summoned.

Once he'd driven away that morning she'd realised how stupid it would be to think of having an affair with him.

Last night must have shaken her more than she'd realised. Either that or Hawke's kisses and his unexpected

106

kindness had scrambled her mind. In the cold light of possible bankruptcy, embarking on an affair with Hawke seemed suicidally dangerous. Hastily she thrust the memory into some hidden, sealed part of her brain; brooding about it would only give him more power.

At Orewa she got out of the car and held out her hand to him, saying in a composed voice, 'Thank you very much for giving me a lift.'

'Any time.' He silenced her with a mocking, heavy-lidded glance before lifting her hand and branding the back of it with the swift touch of his lips.

The smouldering warmth inside her burst into flame, surging up through her skin in a wave of colour. After a brief struggle for control she said smoothly, 'You have such pretty old-fashioned manners, Hawke.'

He released her, smiling appreciatively at her counter-attack. 'My mother will be delighted to know that. I'll see you tonight.'

You will not, she vowed, bolting in to the car hire office. The dazzled receptionist must have been watching through the window; she gave Morna a *Where did you find him?* glance that Morna met with a steely smile.

She was still fuming when she reached the outskirts of Auckland, and that potent combination of indignation and aggression fuelled her actions for the rest of the day.

It was as gruesome as she'd known it was going to be. She'd called each of the clients who'd lost jewellery in the raid. Dealing with the outpourings of anger and sorrow and pain had been exhausting enough.

Then the insurance assessor had arrived. After seeing him out, Morna closed her eyes. He'd been pleasant, but quite definite—because her safe had been left unsecured its contents were not covered. And the owners' insurance would probably not cover their jewellery either.

Which meant that from somewhere she'd have to find an enormous amount of money to repay them. The situation was no worse than she'd anticipated, but it didn't make it any easier to bear.

She looked up when Annie, her assistant, brought in the mail. 'Everything OK out there?' Morna asked. A couple of workmen were dealing with the smashed window.

'I think so.' Annie fidgeted a moment before blurting, 'The police thought I might have left the safe open deliberately.'

'I know,' Morna said honestly. 'But I know you didn't.'

Annie threw her a grateful glance. 'You won't need to sack me—I'll go.'

'Don't be an idiot,' Morna said with crisp conviction. 'I'm not going to sack you. I left the safe open myself once.'

'I'd almost finished locking up when a woman came in and insisted that one of the rings in the window—the emerald princess-cut one—belonged to her.' Annie's hands twisted together as she frowned. 'She said it had been stolen, and that we were a front for the robbers. She just went on and on and on, making wild accusations and calling me a thief and saying she was going to the police.'

Morna nodded. She'd already heard this from the police, but clearly Annie needed to explain.

Annie said on a half-sob, 'In the end she shouted that she would make me pay for stealing the ring, and that I'd better not walk around by myself in the dark. The way she said it, and the way she looked, really scared me. Witless—literally,' she finished with a bleak grimace.

'I don't blame you for being frightened,' Morna said grimly.

'It was ugly and threatening, because it was getting dark by then. I hurried to lock the door behind her and then ran for the bus stop. Morna, I'm so sorry—I just forgot that I hadn't secured the safe.'

'Which was almost certainly the point of the whole exercise,' Morna said wearily. She flinched as one of the workmen replacing the window suddenly broke into song, roaring out a chorus only to be shouted at to stop by his partner.

'I think the police believed me in the end, but I feel so guilty...' Annie's voice trailed away.

Morna got to her feet. 'Stop it. You were set up, and very skilfully.'

'At least you've got insurance,' Annie said, sounding marginally more cheerful.

'We'll manage.' Morna hoped her voice sounded more confident than she felt. She wondered whether she should warn Annie that the shop might have to close, but decided against it until she'd explored every other option.

A small, pretty blonde, Annie had been deeply depressed and penniless when Morna interviewed her for the job. A month previously her husband had left her for her best friend. Morna had followed her instincts and given her the position, and not regretted it for a moment.

The security bell gave its low, melodious peal. Morna grinned at her. 'Get out there and persuade someone to order something hideously expensive!'

Once Annie had gone, Morna flicked through the mail, frowning when she saw a letter from her lawyer. 'What *now*?' she demanded of the universe, ripping the envelope open.

She read the letter inside, then re-read it while she punched numbers into her telephone.

'Could I speak to Mr Partridge, please?' she asked the solicitor's receptionist.

A few seconds later the solicitor came on line. 'Ah, Ms Vause, I rather thought you'd be in contact.'

'What on earth's going on?'

'I'm afraid that I know very little more than you do. As I said in my note, I've received notification from the executor of Mr Jacob Ward's estate to say that they are not satisfied with the proof of Patrick Ward's death. As you know, he was supposed to have been killed in a war in some African country.' He made it sound like an outer planet somewhere in a distant galaxy.

Morna said slowly, 'Jacob—his father—was convinced he'd died.'

'Being convinced is not quite the same thing as documentary proof. Which is what the executor of Mr Ward's will is seeking.'

She stared down at the letter. 'If he died in a war in Africa, is there likely to be the sort of proof that would stand up in court?'

The solicitor's silence was eloquent.

Morna frowned. 'And if there was any possibility at all of him being alive, why on earth did Jacob leave the place to me?'

Mr Partridge gave a dry cough. 'Probably because Mr Ward was, in your words, convinced that his son was dead. After all, he'd prospected in Africa, hadn't he? I imagine he knew the dangers there more than most. I can only assume that there is enough doubt about the circumstances of the so-called death for the executor to want more proof.'

'We'll have to get it settled,' she said quietly. 'I don't want Tarika Bay if Jacob's son is still alive.'

'Don't be so hasty!' The solicitor was horrified. 'I suggest we wait until the executor comes up with proof. If he ever does.'

After Morna hung up she frowned and re-read the letter. If Jacob's son was still alive, the bach was rightfully his.

If he was alive, she hoped he wouldn't sell his father's refuge to Hawke. Head throbbing, she rang and made an appointment with her bank manager.

That done, she went into the workroom. Bankruptcy might be staring her in the face, but she still had work to do.

She filed the end of a length of silver wire into a taper, thrusting it into a hole in the drawplate. Grasping the end with serrated pliers, she applied a rubbing of beeswax and began to pull the wire through. It took time and effort, and as she worked she realised that if Patrick Ward had survived that nasty little war she'd have to move back to Auckland. She was paying very low rent for the bach; anything in Auckland would be infinitely more expensive.

And she'd be moving away from Hawke...

Which would almost certainly be a good thing, she decided stoutly, annealing the wire in the soft edges of the flame, quenching it in pickle and transferring it to the next hole. If she could get away from him she could probably forget him.

In forty years, perhaps.

Had Hawke been with Peri until half an hour before the accident?

'Oh, forget it!' Morna told herself, trying to banish her thoughts in the sheer hard work of drawing down the wire.

A few kisses did not give her any rights where Hawke was concerned. Not that she wanted any rights!

If he touched her again she'd tell him in her coldest voice that she'd accuse him of assault and sexual harassment, instead of melting like a cheap wax candle in humiliating surrender.

*   *   *

The interview with the bank manager had been tense, but although he hadn't agreed to lend her the money she needed, at least he hadn't turned her down. Yet. He'd said it might take a couple of days to go over her figures. And he'd complimented her on her excellent record-keeping.

As she drove home she decided sombrely that she never wanted to endure another day like that. Work hadn't produced its usual satisfaction; although she'd made up the chain, she'd been unable to concentrate on the half-finished pendant she was donating to a charity auction.

So she'd left it and tried to work out a few designs that might suit Peri Carrington's pretty hand, only to come up with trite sketches lacking glamour and finesse.

When she got to the bach Hawke's big Range Rover was parked outside, empty. Stomach clenching, she got out and scanned the empty sand, then headed for the bach. She'd almost reached it when he came strolling around the corner, big and powerful and sleekly graceful in the late-afternoon sun.

Hawke saw her freeze at the sight of him. She didn't glower, but her lush, sexy mouth tightened. Then she gave a little shake of her head and rubbed a hand across her eyes. A surge of protectiveness almost overwhelmed the slow burn of desire.

'Bad day?' he asked.

She shrugged, breasts moving beneath the white silky top. 'Bad enough.'

Instead of unlocking the bach and going inside, she stood still and waited for him to come up, golden eyes cool and distant.

'I've got dinner in the car,' Hawke said evenly.

Her lashes drooped, giving her a sultry, intensely seductive look. 'Then feel free to eat it there,' she said politely.

'Still angry because I kissed your hand?' He smiled at her, a smile edged with self-derision and something else, something that started the blood racing through her body.

'No,' she said shortly.

His brows rose. 'Then it must be because I criticised your clothes.'

'No, you apologised—'

Without giving her time to finish he said reflectively, 'It was ill-bred and discourteous of me, and I can only blame it on a very primitive and—unusual for me—territorial instinct.'

Morna's jaw dropped and she gaped at him. 'What?' she asked stupidly.

He removed the briefcase and suit jacket dangling from her nerveless fingers. 'You heard,' he said pleasantly, and turned her towards the bach with his other hand in the small of her back. 'The thought of other men being able to ogle your glorious body and those long legs brings out an inconvenient possessiveness. I don't enjoy it, but I don't seem to be able to get rid of it. '

'I—' She hesitated, then began again. 'I'm not sure...'

Although he waited courteously for her to continue, her voice trailed into silence and she turned her hot face away from his perceptive gaze. His wry acceptance of his primal maleness should have exasperated her, but some equally primitive female response in her revelled in it.

'You feel it too,' he said with cool relentlessness. 'You watched me at the Hardings' luncheon, and narrowed your eyes when you saw me with Peri last night. It's there, Morna, and all the rationalisation in the world isn't going to drive it away.'

Stalling, she said, 'I need my keys.'

He handed her the briefcase. Their fingers touched and

a charge of electricity ricocheted through her in a sharp, erotic shock. Hiding her face, she bent to open the case.

From above he drawled, 'Of course, we could follow your suggestion.'

'What suggestion?' she asked, unable to prevent a startled look upwards.

Mocking green eyes held hers. 'Pretend it doesn't exist and hope it goes away. Somehow I don't see that working.' When she didn't answer he probed silkily, 'Do you?'

Pulses jumping, Morna hauled out her keys and closed the briefcase. She should be indignant at his bluntness, but all she said as she unlocked the door was, 'I don't poach.'

'And I don't cheat,' he returned in words threaded with steel. 'Peri is the sister of an old friend. She's trying out her wings and I happen to be safe. I'm not saying she won't shed a few tears when she realises her crush on me is going nowhere, but there's nothing romantic between us. I've known her since she was a baby.'

Morna walked into the bach and swung around to face him, clutching her briefcase as though it was a shield. Almost desperately she asked, 'Why are you telling me this?'

'I'm clearing the decks.' He didn't move, and she sensed an implacable will emanating from him. 'It's not at all complicated. I want you, and you want me. We just need to work out what we're going to do about it.'

A complex mixture of elation and apprehension knifed through her. 'Are you always so blunt?' she asked warily.

'I don't see any need for pussyfooting around the inevitable.'

'Which is?'

One black brow lifted. 'Don't be coy, Morna.'

He was proposing an affair. Clearly he thought she was too experienced to want romance and moonshine.

Morna stared down at the hands clamped onto the handle of her case. Capable and strong, their short nails and the small cuts on her fingers revealed that she worked for her living. Peri Carrington's hands had been pampered and manicured.

But Hawke didn't want Peri; he wanted her, Morna Vause.

Except that he didn't know the real Morna Vause. He wanted what he thought her to be, a sophisticated, liberated woman, completely at home with the idea of recreational sex, not one whose sole affair had ended eight years previously.

And, oh God, she wanted him beyond anything she'd ever wanted in her life. If he'd stayed away she might have been able to control the hunger that beat through her in slow, intense waves, swamping her mind with feverish urgency. Now it was impossible.

She said in a brittle voice, 'You have a very practical outlook.'

'If giving you the right to say yes or no without seducing you is practical, then, yes, I have.' A faint note of contempt coloured Hawke's voice. 'Would you rather I swept you off your feet so you can pretend afterwards that you had nothing to do with it?'

Morna winced—because he could do it, and they both knew it. 'I would not!' she retorted with cold distaste.

Glen had done that, seducing her with flowers and dinners and champagne, dazzling her until she'd fallen into his hands like the proverbial ripe plum. And it had all been lies.

Hawke's cynical laugh chilled her. 'I prefer honesty—

from both of us. When we make love it will be because you have made a choice. You'll have no excuses.'

'I don't need an excuse,' she said stiffly.

Without lifting his gaze from hers, he took the briefcase from her fingers and dropped it on the sofa. For the first time she could see beyond the polished jade of his eyes to a sharp, violent hunger.

A reckless need exploded inside her. He was offering her honesty, the right to make her own decisions. He was offering her sex unclouded by emotion. Terrified by the intensity of her desire to take it, she closed her eyes for a second, then opened them and looked at him.

He was watching her, but he made no attempt to move closer. Not even his lashes flickered, yet the impact of his face robbed her of breath.

He wasn't promising her a false love, a lying commitment. This would be a straightforward—even honourable—transaction between them, exchanging passion for passion. He wasn't in love with her.

And she wouldn't be hurt when it finished because she wasn't in love with him.

Yet something wept in the depths of her heart.

Eyes fixed on his face, she said baldly, 'Yes.'

'Yes, what?'

'I prefer honesty too.'

They stood for a second—perhaps longer—in a silence filled with turbulent undercurrents, until Hawke reached for her and pulled her into his arms and held her, his cheek on the dark hot silk of her hair.

'You strip me of every civilised attitude,' he said, his voice harsh and jagged. 'I saw you and I wanted you, and each time I've seen you since I've wanted you more. I dream about you, and wake sweating and hungry because you're not with me. But it's not just that. I like talking to you—you've got an edge to your mind that satisfies me. I want to know you better in every way there is.'

She said quietly, 'I'm not very good at baring my soul.'

Hawke tilted her chin so that he could see into her face. 'I can wait. And when I said that I don't cheat I meant it. I believe in fidelity.'

She believed him. He wasn't like Glen, who'd taken everything she'd had to give and wrecked her on the altar of his own neediness.

'So do I,' she whispered.

Hawke crushed her mouth beneath his. And Morna kissed him back with starving fervour, lost to everything but the power of the moment and the urgent need inflaming her, and the incredible rightness of being in his arms, cocooned in the heat of his hard body as his heart thudded against hers.

Now she realised what she'd missed from their previous kisses. He'd kept his passion on a tight leash—oh, he'd wanted her, but there hadn't been this driven intensity of desire. Now all the barriers were down, all controls splintered; Hawke desired her with the same stark, elemental appetite that sang triumphantly through her.

Mouth vehement against his, she slid her hands beneath his shirt, pulling it free of his belt, and splayed her fingertips over the taut, hot skin of his back, smiling as the muscles corded beneath her touch. Hawke lifted his head and surveyed her flushed face with glittering eyes.

'You've got too many clothes on,' he said between his teeth.

'So have you.' Morna struggled to undo the small pearl button at the top of her shirt, but her fingers shook so much she muttered in frustration.

'Let me,' he said, stopping her with one lean hand over

both of hers, holding them still in a warm grip until they stopped trembling.

Eyes trapped in the burning brightness of his, she nodded and watched his intent face while he undid the buttons and spread out her shirt. The camisole beneath it was no barrier; under his ravenous green gaze her breasts peaked into crests and she shivered, pierced by ravishing delight.

When he'd despatched her shirt she watched dark colour lick along his high, flaring cheekbones. He smiled, slow and wolfish enough to melt the marrow in her bones.

'Do you prefer making love to fully-clothed men?' he asked, his voice low in his throat.

'Not tonight.' She began to undo his shirt, working feverishly because she needed to drown out the warnings from the last rational part of her brain.

Hawke shrugged free of the fabric and lifted her camisole over her head. Her breasts bloomed under his gaze, their peaks thrusting against the sleek fabric of her bra.

He froze. Bewildered, she glanced up into his face and swallowed at the taut hunger that drew the tanned skin tight over the prominent framework.

'You are—beautiful.' He gave a self-derisive smile. 'All I can think of are clichés, but I mean it. You are utterly beautiful. And if I don't get you to a bed I'm going to disgrace myself here and now.'

He unfastened the bra with a practised flick and, without looking at her, picked her up, strode into the bedroom and put her down on the bed. Stunned, Morna had time for two thoughts: she was glad she'd brought her own large bed up from Auckland, and she should have made some attempt to tidy the room that morning.

Then Hawke shucked himself free of the rest of his clothes, and when she saw his splendid, unabashed nakedness her brain shut down in a tidal wave of bold, undiluted lust. A tall, bronzed god of a man, he was perfectly proportioned, his gleaming skin taut over wide shoulders and chest, over lean hips and muscled, horsemen's thighs.

Dry-mouthed, her voice so close to a purr she could have been a tigress, she said, 'So are you…beautiful, I mean.'

'Men are not—'

Shaking her head, she interrupted. 'You are.'

His smile was pure irony, until she sat up and reached for him. That wiped everything but driving desire from his harsh features. Swiftly, without finesse, he came down beside her and kissed her expectant mouth again, a fierce, famished kiss that he broke off too soon with a muttered oath as he tore his lips from hers.

Morna opened dazzled eyes. 'I'm not made of sugar.'

'I know.' But he didn't accept the unspoken invitation; he traced the outline of her mouth with leisurely, confident expertise, and before she had time to do anything but react he moved on to the hollow of her throat. He didn't linger there, either, soon finding the excitable little pulse beneath her ear.

Sensation tore through her like supercharged lightning, an untamed mixture of anticipation and delicious lethargy that robbed the strength from her body while it stimulated it into unbearable pleasure.

She lifted a hand and stroked his chest, her fingertips sensitised to the smooth texture of his skin, and when he dragged in an impeded breath she leaned forward and kissed a spot over his ribs, listening with incandescent joy to the heavy thunder of his heartbeat.

He tasted of salt, and a tangy flavour that was his alone. Morna ached to bury herself in him, to sink deeper and deeper into his essence until they were inseparable. Instead, she licked the skin she'd kissed, and bit it tenderly, and then leaned back and surveyed him from beneath her lashes, her mouth curving into a slow smile.

'Whenever you look at me like that,' he said huskily, 'it's all I can do not to drag you off to the nearest bed.'

'How do I look?' He made her feel beautiful, wanted, able to ask such a question.

'Sultry. Infinitely desirable.' He gave a low laugh. 'I'm astounded you can walk the streets with that mouth and not cause a riot.'

He guided her back onto the pillows and cupped her breast, looking down at the contrast of bronze skin against white. 'Your skin is like silk, and yet you always give an impression of strength,' he said unexpectedly, stroking a thumb across the pleading nipple. 'I like that.'

Fire bloomed in Morna at the caress, gathering force as it swept the length of her to coalesce between her legs in flames. But his words satisfied some secret sorrow, enabling her to say, 'I am strong.' Her voice sank into that throaty purr. 'But not as strong as you...'

She skimmed a hand from his shoulder down to his hip.

A harsh sound erupted from his throat and he bent his head to her breast. As his mouth closed around the eager peak she moaned, twisting restlessly at the exquisite sensation that clenched every muscle in her body.

Shattered by the ferocity of her response, she clamped her legs together, pressing the need in. Sighing, she held him close, and exulted at the erotic friction of his mouth on her skin.

It wasn't meant to be like this—she should struggle for control instead of yielding to this sensual fever. Yet thought was impossible, drowned by sensuous craving as Hawke worked carnal magic on her with his skilled mouth and knowledgeable hands until she moaned again with reckless excitement.

She almost sobbed with frustration when he eased away to lift her slightly and unzip her skirt, sliding it down her legs before tossing it onto the floor.

Hawke saw the tell-tale signals of passion in her face, and shuddered at the merciless hunger that poured through him. She lay on the bed like a captive of her own desire, her glorious hair spilling in a night-black flood around her wild face and across her shoulders. The last rays of the sun kindled fire from her hair and tinted her skin with a soft, fugitive colour.

Her breasts, high and lusciously curved, pouted above a narrow waist that subtly invited an exploration of the delights beneath her sheer tights. Although her whisky-coloured eyes were half closed and slumbrous, they stayed fixed on his face with smouldering intensity as one thud closely followed by another, told him she'd kicked off her shoes.

'I've seen you like this in my dreams,' he said, the words torn from some primal matrix that subverted all the shackles he'd learned to put on his tongue and his mind.

When her lashes flickered he knew with a jolt of savage satisfaction that she'd dreamed of him too.

Gathering up her slim, vibrant body in his arms, Hawke kissed the shallow indentation of her navel before easing the tights free of her hips.

His mouth followed his hands. With it he discovered the contours of her hips and the slight curve of her stomach. Then he straightened to lie beside her. Morna stared into his buccaneer's face, her heart thudding crazily in her ears.

'You look like a virgin,' he said unsteadily.

Her voice shook. 'How does a virgin look?'

'Unsure of herself.' He measured the sweep of her cheekbones. 'Innocently seductive.' He opened his hand around her square chin, then traced the outline of the lips that clung to his fingertip. 'Beyond desire,' he finished on a raw note that spoke subtly of something deeper than passion.

A shock of joy exploded inside her like a nova. Her voice trembled. 'I'm not a virgin.'

'Neither am I.' It was like a vow, deep and intense, the tone transcending the words.

And the joy in Morna blazed like light through the darkness, because she read more than a momentary passion in the blazing green eyes, in his smile, in the gentleness of his touch.

Her lips closed on the tip of his finger, but this time her teeth clenched on the skin.

'You want to bite?' he asked, and kissed her again.

Drugged with sensuality, her hips pushing against his loins, Morna opened her mouth to the importunate demands of his. Passion emptied out her mind, leaving nothing but the need to make love to him, to take him inside her and know him completely.

Not, she realised dimly, just sexually; that thought should scare her into instant rejection, but in Hawke's arms she had room only for desire.

CHAPTER NINE

'WAIT,' Hawke said harshly, and turned to the side of the bed.

Aching with violent frustration, Morna devoured every smooth movement of his body, from the power and width of his shoulders down the flexible line of his spine to the narrow hips. Dusk seeped into the room, mysterious with the promise of night. She could feel the weave of the bedspread against her back and her legs, the movements of the mattress as he swung back to face her.

Deep, deep inside her something shattered into shards. She smiled and reached out her arms to draw him down to her and over her and into her.

Resisting, he stroked the sensitive spot between her legs. Morna bit back a cry. Hot impatience stormed through her like a war-band intent on plunder; opening her legs and lifting her hips, she silently invited him in.

'All right?' he asked, darkening eyes searching her face.

'Better than all right.' Her voice emerged in a strained whisper. She linked her hands around his shoulders, and offered her mouth and her body.

While their mouths were joined Hawke completed the link with one hard thrust that propelled her into another dimension where sensation ruled. Morna's arms locked around him as she clenched her internal muscles to hold him there. Slowly, so slowly it was torment, he withdrew, then took her again, and this time she cried out a jagged syllable—his name—at the frenzied pleasure that sky-rocketed through her.

As though that soft cry had snapped some chain of discipline, he flung his head back and took her with over-powering eroticism. Morna's eyes closed, thoughts scattering like spindrift before a storm, violent tension clamping her body in silken fetters as he thrust into her, taking her as completely as she took him. Waves of sexual excitement drove her higher and higher until she stiffened beneath him, finally reaching some unreachable place in a starburst of rapturous sensation.

Almost instantly Hawke joined her in that place, and his explosive release sent her soaring again into the realm of heat and ecstatic sensory overload.

But when she'd made a lovely, leisurely descent, and their breathing had settled, Hawke moved to lift himself from her.

Morna's arms tightened around his back. 'No. Not yet.'

'I'm too heavy.' His voice was low and rough, but in spite of his words he stayed.

'You're not. I'm strong, remember?'

Enveloped by his heat, his scent a passionate incitement, she luxuriated in bliss beneath the big body pressing her down into the mattress. Lazy satisfaction drained her energy, yet she felt more alert, more alive than she ever had before.

So that was what it was like—fire and wild sweetness, piercing pleasure and utter, ravishing completion.

Yet slowly, from out of nowhere, a vague, formless chill invaded Morna's mind.

Hawke said, 'However strong you are, you must be uncomfortable.'

Before she could protest he turned onto his side and, with the deftness of someone who had done it many times before, pulled her to lie half across him with her face on his chest and her head tucked under his chin.

Locked in that reassuring embrace, her mind still whirling with wonder, her body lax and pleasured to the utmost, Morna fought her growing foreboding with logic.

This fulfilment might be new to her, but it wasn't to him. She'd recognised his experience the moment she'd seen him; that air of sexual confidence was unmistakable.

And she'd been right. Sex with Hawke had proved one thing: he was a stud. Alpha male to the limit. Although she'd loved Glen, she'd never felt anything like this transcendent experience.

Because it seemed crass to compare Hawke with another man when she was lying in his arms after making love—no, after fantastic sex, she corrected herself hastily—she concentrated on monitoring the way his heartbeat steadied and slowed. She noticed when his breathing eased back into regularity, and the subtle difference to his scent.

Eau de sated male, she thought wearily, and quite suddenly dropped into sleep.

She woke to darkness and unusual stiffness, the savoury scent of food and the unexpected rattle of her stomach. For a moment she wondered where on earth she was, until it all came back. After a frozen second she sprinted out of the tangled remnants of the bed and into the bathroom, only pausing to snatch her robe on the way.

She emerged with a scrubbed, gleaming body, combed hair, and an attitude. Sounds of movement in the kitchen sent her scurrying into jeans and a loose jersey top; she slicked a gloss of colour onto her mouth, wincing at the tender, full contours.

It took every scrap of self-possession she owned to stroll out of the bedroom. Although she moved noiselessly and Hawke was standing with his back to her in the kitchen, she hadn't taken a second step into the room before he turned.

Her chin lifted and she met his eyes with more than a hint of defiance.

He smiled. 'You look rested,' he said, and held out a glass of champagne. 'You'll feel even better when you've had something to eat.'

Well, why shouldn't he be casual and charming? Nothing stupendous had happened to him—he was used to such occasions! Accepting the glass, Morna sipped from it, colouring when he bent to kiss her.

'Tastes good,' he murmured, green eyes glinting above a wicked smile as he stepped back.

'So does this lovely wine,' she said, hiding the quiver in her voice with smile.

'I'm glad you like it.' He lifted his own glass and toasted her, then turned back to the stove to stir something on one of the elements.

Keeping her eyes on the bench, now laden with dishes, she took another quick sip before asking, 'Where did all this delicious-smelling food come from? Surely you didn't cook it?'

He laughed. 'I'm no expert in the kitchen. I got the chef at the resort to put something together. Have I gone down in your estimation?'

It was a rhetorical question; men with his inbuilt self-assurance didn't really care what others thought of them. No doubt he knew his prowess in bed outranked any culinary skill.

'I'm too hungry to care who cooked it,' she told him truthfully, and put the glass down. 'I'll set the table.'

The meal was magnificent. As Morna forked up the last of the scallop and noodle salad he'd served for the first course Hawke leaned back in his chair and asked, 'What made you decide to be a jeweller?'

'Oh, that was easy.' She gave a reminiscent smile. 'When Nick was at boarding school—'

'Boarding school? Did he get a scholarship?'

Heat singed her cheekbones, but Morna kept her gaze and her voice steady. 'Glen Spencer met him one day and decided he had great potential, so he used his influence to get him into his old school. When Nick had a weekend off he'd come back and take me window-shopping. We'd go into bookshops—we spent hours there until someone chased us out because we read but didn't buy. Nick didn't fancy admiring the latest fashions, so we'd look in jewellery shop windows. I fell in love with the colour and gleam and the—oh, the opulence and glory, and the sheer romantic magic of the stones themselves.'

Watching her face, the sultry marks of passion overlaid by a lively vitality, Hawke wondered if the romance and glamour of gemstones had been the sole link between her and Jacob Ward.

He thought of the information he'd been given that day, information that hinted at the possibility of Jacob's son surviving the war he'd been caught up in.

If it turned out to be true, what would Morna do when the man arrived in New Zealand? Give up Tarika Bay, or cling to it?

And why, if she was the mercenary, calculating woman he'd assumed, had she returned to sell the Bay?

His mouth tightened as he watched her sip her wine, red lips lushly inviting. For a while—OK, since the day they'd met!—he'd been fighting a desire to find excuses for her supposed avarice. She'd said she wouldn't sell the Bay because Jacob Ward hadn't wanted him to have it.

Perhaps she'd taken Glen Spencer's money because she felt he owed her.

As the bastard did. Pity he was dead—Hawke would have enjoyed telling him with cold precision exactly what he thought of him. She'd only been twenty-one when she'd become his lover, and he'd got rid of her with a brutality that still shocked Hawke's informant.

Then there was the question of the unlocked safe and its contents. He'd made a couple of telephone calls about that, and it seemed Morna would have to reimburse the clients who had lost their jewellery.

He put his fork down on his empty plate. Now he found himself wondering whether her wild abandonment in his arms had been natural generosity or a calculating attempt to soften him in case she needed a loan. The thought outraged him for reasons he wasn't prepared to explore right then.

It would be much simpler if he could convince himself that she was a greedy, amoral sensualist.

He heard the reservation in his tone as he said, 'So you decided to make a career in jewellery design.'

She lifted her glass, but set it back down with the wine untasted. 'That came later. First of all I did an apprenticeship as a jeweller.'

'It's a career that's an interesting combination of creativity and craftsmanship. I think I envy you.'

Her quick glance revealed astonishment, immediately hidden by her long lashes. In a remote voice she said, 'It's very absorbing.'

Something in her still reserve warned him he'd inadvertently touched a sore spot. Glen Spencer, he thought with a flash of insight as he recalled someone telling him that she'd stopped working when she'd lived with the older man.

Did she expect him to have the same prejudices and insecurities as her first lover? Only a man with an extremely fragile ego would make such a demand of a woman with talent like hers.

A sudden need to force her to recognise that he was nothing like Spencer burned in his gut, but he controlled it enough to content himself with reaching out to touch her hand.

Remorseless hunger gripped him when he saw the breath stop in her throat and the swift flame of heat along her superb cheekbones—signs she could neither hide nor control. Whether or not she intended to ask him for money, she wanted him.

It took brutal self-control not to suggest that they ignore the rest of dinner and go back into that shabby bedroom. All he could think of was sinking himself into her sinuous, sleek heat again and again until both of them were too exhausted to do anything but sleep.

Because he couldn't touch her and not want her, he removed his hand and picked up his glass. And because he trusted neither his voice nor his will-power, he said nothing.

She filled the silence. 'That was lovely—your chef's a genius. I'll stack the dishes.' Without looking at him, she carried the plates across to the bench.

Coldly furious with himself, Hawke got to his feet. He'd never had to worry about loss of control before, and it infuriated him that this woman should be the one to force him so close to the edge.

Perhaps it was simply that she had enough contradictions in her character to intrigue him. Businesswoman, artist and craftsperson, sensual lover yet a woman who blushed occasionally and hated it...

She had certainly enjoyed making love with him, but did it mean anything to her?

Dangerous question; always before he'd asked no more than that his lovers wanted him and enjoyed what they shared. He swore silently as his body hardened. Calling it to order, he tipped rocket leaves into a bowl and scattered shavings of parmesan cheese across them.

Yet another question came back to taunt him; she ate with delicate sensuality, flirted with skill and discretion, and certainly knew how to make a man pay attention to her.

So why did she make love like a virgin?

Once more his body betrayed him as he remembered her passion—and the surprise she hadn't been able to hide when she went to pieces in his arms. Surely that wasn't the first time she'd reached a climax?

For some reason he found himself hoping it was. Strutting your stuff, he thought in icy self-contempt. Perhaps she was simply a very clever actress, all things to all men.

Morna scanned the hard angles of his face and wondered what he was thinking. 'Can I take something across to the table?' she asked.

He indicated a casserole with the savoury odour of chicken and herbs emanating from it. 'I'll bring the rest.'

Once seated again, and with the meal served, Morna said on a sigh, 'I think I might be in love with your chef.'

'Bad luck for him,' Hawke said blandly. 'I'll have to sack him.'

She laughed, although a chill of unease lurked beneath her amusement. 'Cathy told me that you'd just come back from Central Africa,' she said. 'Were you on safari?'

'A business trip. I have a friend there who's trying to start a beef industry, crossing local cattle with imported breeds. It's a pet project of mine.'

Interested, she asked more questions. He seemed surprised, but needed little encouragement to segue into a description of the country he'd just been to. A clear thinker, he was pragmatic when it came to the political and educational handicaps his project suffered, but when he spoke of the people and the land his voice warmed and he conveyed their dramatic appeal more potently than any television documentary she'd ever seen.

Afterwards, still talking, they washed up. What now? Did he expect to spend the night here?

She glanced out of the window at the beach, shimmering beneath a radiant moon, and asked casually, 'Would you like to go for a walk? I ate a bigger dinner than usual, and it's a glorious night.'

Hawke glanced at her, eyes cool as glacier water. 'Why not?' he said easily.

They strolled along the sand, not talking much as the moon sailed across the depthless sky and blotted out the stars with its radiance.

When Morna shivered Hawke slipped an arm around her shoulders, hugging her into the warmth and protection of his big body. 'Let's go back in.'

Once inside he said, 'Running scared, Morna? If you don't want me to stay, all you have to do is tell me.'

She bit her lip, but decided on honesty. 'It's not that I don't want you to stay.'

'But?' He wasn't angry yet he wanted an answer.

'I need time to myself,' she said unsteadily. 'This—this morning I had no idea...' She was stopped by his sardonic gaze.

'Of course you did,' he said, and when she flushed he flicked her cheek and smiled. 'It's all right,' he said smoothly. 'I'll see you tomorrow.'

'Probably not—I've got a lot to do.' And she did need

time—time and space. Something had happened, something she didn't understand, and she had to work out what it was. Giving in to temptation would cloud her mind in a haze of sensuality, drawing her further and further down a path that threaded its way through hidden dangers.

He gave her a long judicial look that almost made her squirm. 'Help me carry out the dishes to the car,' he suggested.

Once the dishes had been packed into the Range Rover, he looked across at her hired car. 'How's it going?'

'Good.' Far more comfortable than the old one, but frighteningly expensive. She bit her lip; during the evening she'd managed to forget the threat hanging over her, but it was back now, gnawing at her peace.

Hawke said, 'And how did you get on with the assessor?'

'All right,' she said with careful composure, adding wryly, 'Suspicious, of course, but fair.'

'Insurance assessors are paid to be suspicious. Don't worry about him,' Hawke said laconically, turning her into his arms.

For a moment he looked down into her face, his own almost stern. Morna shivered, and he said, 'You're getting cold again,' and kissed her with stark hunger that almost changed her decision to send him home.

But he dropped his arms and stepped away, so she didn't humiliate herself by begging him to stay. 'Morna,' he said, his voice deep and lingering as he said her name.

'Yes?'

He laughed, and said, 'Just—Morna. Goodnight,' and got into the Range Rover.

Her name meant *Beloved*.

'Don't be such an utter idiot!' she scolded, watching the rear lights head up the drive before she went back to the bach. That kiss had done exactly what he'd intended it to—reminded her of the passion they'd shared. 'Love doesn't come into this.'

She stopped at the doorway to the bedroom, staring at the wrecked bed. A small guilty smile banished her frown. Making love to Hawke had been extraordinary, beyond anything she'd ever experienced. He'd been passionate and sensual and overwhelming, and the pleasure had been almost unbearable.

He was everything a woman could ask of a lover— more, because beneath the fire and hunger and intolerable ecstasy she thought there had been tenderness.

Of course, she could be trying to fool herself into thinking she meant more to him than a quick, satisfying tumble in the hay.

Shivering, she remade the bed. She felt as though she'd somehow been hurled into a different universe, one with different laws, different values. It scared her that she'd watched him leave with an awful emptiness in her heart.

After Glen had dumped her she'd vowed never to let herself rely on any man again. But as she curled up in a chair in the darkened living room and watched the moon-path over the sea, chills raced across the skin Hawke and kissed and caressed, and tears burned behind her eyes.

'Morna?'

Frowning, Morna cut off the LPG torch and swung around to see Annie hovering just inside the workroom door. 'What is it?' she asked, putting down the ring she was working on.

'Someone wants to see you.' Annie opened her eyes wide and fanned her face with her hand.

Morna's heart thudded into overdrive. It was two days

since she'd seen Hawke—but why would he come here?
'Who?'

'Don't know, but he's male and ab-so-*lute*-ly heroic.'
This time Annie rolled her eyes. 'And he's not going
away.'

Morna glanced at her stained hands. They looked awful—and it would take too long to clean them. 'OK, I'll
come out,' she said, getting up.

Her heart flipped when she saw him, lean and dangerous in a dark business suit and filled with enough potent
male magnetism to make her carefully decorated salon
seem frivolous and brittle. He was examining a diamond
and platinum pendant on a platinum chain that had been
a brute to make.

Now she was glad she'd stuck with it.

When she closed the door behind her he turned and
scanned her face with cool, perceptive eyes—eyes that
rested a moment on her hands. 'Bad time?' he asked.

'I was working, but it's all right.' Ridiculous to be so
formal when the last time—oh, better not even think about
the last time she'd seen him!

'Come to lunch with me.'

She waved her grimy fingers at him. 'It will take me
more than five minutes to deal with these,' she said wryly,
'and even then they won't be entirely clean.'

'So?' He held out his hand.

Oddly unsure, she put hers in it, bracing herself for the
familiar charge of electricity. For the past two lonely days
she'd wondered if making love would blunt that fierce
edge; instead it seemed to have honed it. Now she knew
how tender his hands could be on a woman's skin—how
tender, and then how suddenly rough...

Her stomach clenched.

He examined her short nails and the grime. 'My mother

is a gardener,' he said calmly. 'She won't use gloves—she says they stop her from working properly—so she can never get the stains out from beneath her nails. It doesn't worry her.' He ran her sensitive fingertips across his callused palm. 'The signs of hard work have their own beauty.'

Morna looked up with a quick, wicked smile. 'Appreciated only by workers and fellow-gardeners,' she said. 'I'll be out in ten minutes.'

Anticipation bubbled as she scrubbed away at her skin in her small washroom; an industrial strength cleaner removed most of the grime, and losing the top layer of skin with it was a small price to pay. She smoothed on hand cream and groped in her bag for her lipstick.

He'd come for her. It probably meant nothing, but she couldn't help hoping that it was an omen.

Of what? Lipstick in hand, she froze, and stared at herself in the mirror with wary foreboding. As long as she kept her head she'd be safe. This was an affair, sweet and simple. Well, perhaps not sweet, she conceded with a secret smile.

She wasn't going to fall into the trap of thinking that sex would lead to love. Hawke Challenger might be the most magnificent man she'd ever come across, but falling in love with him would be like jumping out of a plane without a parachute. He was peril on two legs—walking, talking sexual dynamite—and any woman who tried to chain him was going to have her work cut out.

At least, unlike Glen, he didn't want an adoring younger woman to bolster his ego.

But perhaps he enjoyed the idea of a sophisticated, experienced older woman...

CHAPTER TEN

THE thought sliced through Morna's anticipation like a poisonous dart. Sickened, she stopped touching up the colour on her lips and leaned forward. Yes, there they were—the tiny lines around her mouth and eyes, inevitable indications of her age.

After a second she shrugged. Hawke had lines too—fans at the corners of his eyes from long hours spent in the sun, laughter lines around his beautiful mouth.

And anyway, in a relationship based on straight, uncommitted sex, age didn't matter.

Except that it did, she admitted, combing her hair into its smooth bob. But he enjoyed more than the sex; he'd said he liked her smart mouth and her mind. Counting over the compliments as though they were her most precious gems, she straightened the black V-necked jacket over her long trousers. A rapid change from her comfortable shoes to a pair of high-heeled sandals finished her preparations and she left the tiny cloakroom with her head held high.

Out in the showroom Annie was fluttering up at Hawke, slim body eagerly angled towards him, pert, pretty face alive with excitement. Although his smile was more tolerant than flirtatious, it still loosed a nasty twist of jealousy in Morna's heart.

It eased when he looked up the moment she opened the door. His indulgent smile vanished, and she felt his awareness, sinfully exotic and shot with intense undertones.

When he said her name it was like a caress; Morna

shivered as the sound reached down inside her and melted every last shred of resistance.

Somehow he'd managed to find parking only a few metres along the street. Not the Range Rover—this was the car he'd been driving the night he'd run her off the road.

Once in it, he said, 'I thought we'd go to Mil's,' naming an upmarket restaurant.

Morna kept her eyes away from her hands. 'If you think they can handle me in my working clothes,' she said lightly.

'They've handled me in my working clothes frequently,' he said drily, starting the car.

'The mind boggles!'

He laughed. 'This is as much a working outfit as moleskins and a checked shirt. And if the state of your hands worries you, why do you make your own jewellery?'

'It's very important to me that the final product fulfils my initial vision for the piece.'

He shot a too perceptive glance sideways before deftly avoiding a woman in a tiny scarlet shopping basket of a car, who was apparently intent on suicide by vehicle. 'I suspected as much. You're a perfectionist.'

'I suppose so,' she admitted, realising that the shiny emotion inside her was happiness. 'But not obsessive, I hope. I'm never entirely satisfied with what I do, but trying for perfection each time keeps me honest.'

He nodded, and remarked, 'The shop doesn't look like it's been raided.'

'They fixed it completely the next day.'

She hoped her voice didn't show any signs of withdrawal. The bank had come through with a loan, but her enormous relief was tempered by the stringent conditions. She'd signed a contract that would keep her in even tighter straits than before, but at least she'd fulfilled her obligations to the clients who'd lost their jewellery.

Unfortunately, to meet the terms she'd no longer be able to pay instalments of Glen's legacy to her charity, which meant even more years before she was free.

But she wasn't going to worry about that now. Live for the day, she decided, admiring the dark cloth of Hawke's suit. 'Have you been to a meeting?'

'Yes.' He turned into a car park. 'And I've got another this afternoon, followed by dinner with a government minister who wants to pick my brains, but will ignore anything I suggest that might offend or upset the smallest segment of the electorate.'

She said brightly, 'So I'm the light relief?'

After backing the car into place, Hawke switched off the engine and turned his head, heavy eyelids dropping to almost hide the green gleam in his eyes. Morna's breath locked in her throat. She had the odd idea that this was an extremely important moment.

'More like the reward,' he said with a twist of his lips.

It wasn't the right answer, but there was no right answer, so she had no reason to feel a stab of disappointment.

She masked it with a fugitive grin, all come-hither mischief.

Hawke's eyes blazed pure emerald-green, and he laughed deep in his throat. 'I'd like to take you home now and spend the rest of the afternoon with you, but it's not going to happen.'

'Not for me, anyway.' Her heartbeat sped up and colour burned across her cheekbones. 'I've got a commission to finish.'

They ate lunch in an atmosphere of sexual tension so strong that Morna couldn't remember the food, or even what they talked about. That afternoon she had to force herself to concentrate, and instead of staying late she left only half an hour behind Annie, driving though a crystalline autumn evening that faded rapidly towards dusk as she neared home.

She tried to watch the television news; when that failed to keep her attention she picked up a book. After repeating the same page three times she closed it and got angrily to her feet, striding out onto the timber deck to listen to the sea breathing slowly onto the beach.

No bird called; the only lights she could see were tiny pinpricks further up the coast. Goaded by restlessness, she went out to walk in the cold white light of the moon, tramping over Hawke's land as though somehow she could connect to him.

So this was what infatuation was like...

Because it had to be infatuation—the alternative was impossible.

Back home she ran a bath in an attempt to soothe the fever in her blood. She'd just got out when she heard an engine, and saw lights coming down the hill.

Excitement exploded inside her like a nova. After rapidly blotting her wet body, she wrapped the towel around herself and raced to the door, opening it as Hawke raised his hand to knock.

Without speaking he stepped inside, kicked the door shut behind him and leaned back on it to examine her bare shoulders and long legs with narrowed, hot eyes. The arrogant framework of his face stood out sharply and his smile was a dark promise.

Although Morna's skin burned, she didn't hesitate or back off. 'Was the dinner boring?' she asked huskily.

'Not as bad as I'd expected, but it was nowhere near as interesting as you.' Winding through his thickened voice she heard a raw hunger that set fire to the weary warnings of her mind.

She walked towards him, lifting her face for his kiss. His arms closed around her with gratifying speed and strength, but he didn't accept that mute invitation. Looking up into his hard, gorgeous face, she wondered at the sudden edge of steel in the pale green eyes.

'No more reservations?' he asked.

He was too astute. But somehow during that interminable afternoon she'd crossed over a line she'd drawn in the sand years before in a surrender she wasn't prepared to examine yet.

'No more,' she conceded, her own voice low and uneven.

'Smile at me,' he commanded, and when she did he said, 'You smile like a sinful angel,' and kissed her with a driven intensity that summoned an equal response from her.

That night Morna learned how much a man could demand from her—and how much pleasure she could experience without dying of rapture. Hawke taught her that her body could be an instrument of the keenest sensitivity that responded to his caresses with mindless, helpless passion.

And she learned how to touch him so that he trembled against her, and that surrender could be a two-way thing.

Towards morning he said in a voice that echoed in her soul, 'Sleep now.'

And she learned that the sleep that comes when locked in a man's arms is the sweetest sleep of all.

'Horses are absolutely not my thing,' Morna said firmly, repressing a shudder.

'Have you ever been on one?' Hawke asked with a lazy smile.

'No.'

'So how do you know they're not your thing?'

She glowered at him. 'I hate it when you're logical.'

And because he was too overpowering, in a green polo shirt that turned his eyes to darkest jade and trousers that hugged his long, heavily muscled legs, she transferred her gaze to the chestnut mare. 'Look, you can tell she doesn't like me.'

'She knows you're scared.' His smile turned her bones to custard.

'I'm not scared,' she said indignantly. 'I'm cautious—especially when it comes to creatures that are bigger than me.'

'You've spent your life being scared,' he said, and cut short her protests. 'OK, I'll make a bargain with you.'

'What sort of bargain?' She was terrified he'd realise that he had only to ask her and she'd do anything for him. 'And caution is not the same thing as fear!'

He ignored that defiant final statement. 'Give Princess a try, and if you really don't like riding her I'll never ask you to try again.'

'Princess? It's not exactly an original name, is it?'

'A young cousin named her,' he said indifferently. 'Stop avoiding the issue. What's it to be?'

Morna chewed her lip and eyed the horse. It flicked its ears at her and made a pleasant, composed whuffling noise. Compared to the enormous black thing that Hawke rode, it seemed small and reasonably controllable. 'Done,' she said briskly.

They shook on it—a handshake that somehow turned into a kiss, followed by more, until Hawke let her go and said accurately, 'Stop trying to inveigle me back into bed.'

She gave him a sultry, inviting smile. Late the previous night he'd returned from a short business trip to Singapore; neither of them had slept much.

Although the familiar green fire kindled in the depths of his eyes, he said, 'OK, put on the helmet and I'll give you a leg up.'

For someone who had probably been born in the saddle, he was formidably patient with her, and as Princess behaved with the regal dignity promised by her name Morna began to relax.

'Great,' Hawke said, smiling down at her from his monstrous beast. 'You've got a natural grace that I knew would help. See, Princess is much more relaxed now too.'

Morna sighed. 'You'll have me bungee-jumping next,' she said morosely.

'Only if you want to,' he returned, his tone deep and lazily amused.

She grinned. 'Already done it. Loved it! Have you?'

'Not yet.' He was laughing. 'Are you going to insist I leap off a bridge in return for persuading you to ride?'

'Only if you want to,' she said solemnly, her heart warming because it seemed that he was thinking of a— well, not a future exactly, but some time together.

The past month had been heavenly, as though somehow they'd been able to opt out of the constraints of time and circumstance and lose themselves in a world where only they existed.

Dazed by happiness, Morna was too content coasting in this passionate idyll to worry about the future. Not even a call from her solicitor relaying information from the trustee of Jacob's estate had concerned her; apparently there did seem to be reasonable doubt about his son's death. Patrick Ward might have disappeared into one of the invading army's prisons.

'But don't concede anything until—or unless—they come up with proof,' Mr Partridge cautioned her.

Lost in her cocoon of delight, Morna had ignored the prospect of having to move from Tarika Bay. Hawke spent his spare time at the bach, grumbling occasionally about the discomfort of furniture made for standard-sized people. Although he could cook a basic repertoire of dishes, mostly he arrived with meals prepared by his chef, so they picnicked on delicious food.

They talked, exploring personalities, discovering each other's tastes and values. He made her laugh, and she teased him; they argued about world affairs and cryptic crosswords and the latest books and old music.

And they made love.

Morna stared ahead through her horse's ears. As always, when she thought of the hours she'd spent in Hawke's arms, heat began to build inside her and her skin tightened in delicious recollection. One of the mare's ears turned back as though she could sense the nuances of Morna's pleasure.

'You were right,' she said abruptly, looking up at Hawke. 'I am enjoying this. Don't you dare say I told you so.'

'I wouldn't dream of it,' he said solemnly.

'How long do you have to spend riding before you look as though you and the horse are one animal?'

He shrugged. 'Some people never get there.' He laughed at the determination in her face. 'Perfectionist. You won't be happy until you've managed it.'

'Like you, I prefer to do things well,' she said with demure provocation.

They ambled on until they came to a big paddock that stretched along the top of a ridge with spectacular views out over the Hauraki Gulf and down to Auckland.

Hawke's black horse had been showing signs of res-
tiveness, and Hawke said now, 'I'll take him for a run.
Just keep Princess headed in the same direction.'

She bit her lip, but when the mare showed no signs of
thundering after them she relaxed and watched Hawke and
his horse.

This romantic interlude would end sometime, she knew,
and when it did she'd cope. The only problem was that
she suspected she was beginning to like him too much.

Not love him—never that.

'Been there, done that,' she told Princess, who oblig-
ingly did the neat trick with her ear again.

Liking was a far more solid thing than the long-ago
emotion she'd felt for Glen.

Looking back, she could see that she'd been dazzled
into believing that she loved him; he'd targeted her because she was young and easily influenced. And that said
a lot about Glen, and something about her too. She'd
probably been looking for the father she'd never had.

She watched Hawke and the gelding take a wide turn
at the far end of the paddock and begin back at a more
moderate pace. The warm autumn sun washed lovingly
over the man and his horse, highlighting Hawke's dark
hair and the gleaming hide of the animal.

A sharp, unknown emotion stabbed Morna. 'And this?'
she asked beneath her breath. 'What's Hawke? The
younger brother you never had? A passing fling with a
toy boy?' The complete absurdity of that idea set a sardonic smile flickering across her lips.

The mare whickered, stretching out her stride a bit.
'Don't even think about it,' Morna advised her, recalling
Hawke's instructions and tightening her fingers a little on
the reins.

No, the last thing she'd been looking for was a passionate interlude with a virile younger stud. She'd just tumbled headlong into lust, and instead of sating it with lovemaking she'd become addicted. And when he moved on, as he would, she'd have to go cold turkey.

It would be painful. Wonderful though the sex was, she'd miss a lot more than that—his keen, incisive mind and his dry humour, the sense of security when he was with her, something she thought of as rightness, of dove-tailing…

But she'd relinquish him with more grace than she had Glen, she thought grimly. She was a lot older, and much more sensible than she had been then.

That night they attended a ball, one organised to fund research on the illness that had killed Morna's mother. Hawke had asked her to go with him, and as she'd donated a trinket for auction she'd accepted.

Dressed in a silk satin dress she'd hired, she looped a topaz and diamond pendant from the shop over her head and settled it between the shoestring straps. She carefully applied mascara and eyeliner, blended on a smudge of shadow that turned her eyes to golden gems, and chose red, red lipstick.

And decided the dress was worth its hire fee.

When she opened the door to Hawke her heart leapt in her breast. Although she'd seen him in superbly cut suits, nothing had prepared her for his impact in black and white.

Dry-mouthed, she said, 'Formal evening dress was designed for men like you.'

Tension shimmering between them, he gave her a hot, hooded scrutiny. 'And you always look magnificent. What made you decide to wear a colour?'

Flushing, she looked down at the topaz silk. 'I liked it,' she said simply.

'So do I.' His voice was smoky with desire. 'I suppose we have to go?'

'Yes,' Morna said beneath her breath. 'Yes, we have to go. I've made a pendant for the auction.'

He showed his teeth in a smile that held little humour. 'In that case I'd better not touch you.'

And the fever of anticipation in the pit of her stomach began to build. It kept doing so through an eternal evening; every word, every glance, every touch when they danced combined to consume her with need. Morna sat through speeches without hearing a word, saw the pendant she'd donated sell for about twice what it was worth in a bidding frenzy whipped up by the well-known media personality who acted as MC, and all the time was only really aware of the man who never left her side.

He was, she realised painfully, becoming too important to her.

She had a decision to make—was it better to end it now, or should she hope for a miracle? Cowardice whispered for an immediate end, but newly discovered hope sang a soft siren song in her heart.

Eventually Hawke said under his breath, 'Let's get out of here.'

Morna nodded. She'd had enough of women caressing him with their eyes, of men who shook his hand in obvious respect, of people who watched him with avid interest—and her with speculation. She longed to go home with him, yet because she suspected that from now on home for her would be wherever Hawke was she was afraid.

However, tonight would be theirs.

When he turned into the resort, she looked at him with surprise. In a slow drawl that didn't hide the rasp beneath the words, he said, 'It's closer.'

'Only five minutes.' She tried to laugh, but it emerged on a low, husky note that only underlined the taut atmosphere in the car.

'I've been waiting all evening,' he told her in the flinty tone of desperate restraint. 'I believed that patience was my strong suit, but you've managed to destroy that.'

This was dangerous, she thought, shivering at the subtle alteration to the sexual tension that had linked them right from the start.

Except in bed with her, he'd always been self-contained, disciplined. Tonight she sensed that his iron control had worn paper-thin. A heated languor tightened her skin and sent shivers of excitement prickling through her.

The autumn chill meant that no one was outside to see them drive through the resort, although music still echoed from behind lighted windows in the main building.

Hawke parked the car in the garage and leaned over to open the door for Morna. He didn't touch her, not then—and not when they went into the darkened house. She'd been there often enough to be able to find her way around, which was just as well because Hawke didn't turn on any lights.

In the dark sitting room he turned and pulled her into his arms. 'I'd hoped to make it to the bedroom,' he said, the last word muffled against her lips.

Eventually he lifted his head and said in a harsh, indistinct voice, 'And I'm going to. I want to see you take this pretty thing off.'

She opened her mouth to say something and he added, 'With the light on.'

'I want that too,' she said ridiculously.

He let her go and stepped back. Morna felt his reluctance, as tangible as hers. Walking sedately, her knees wobbly and her mouth still tingling from the force and passion of that kiss, she went with him into his bedroom.

Hawke switched on a lamp beside the enormous bed and surveyed her with a hunger so uncompromising Morna's bones went limp.

In a hard-edged, unsettling voice he said, 'I've been watching you all evening in that lovely, wicked dress, wanting to get you out of it, but now you're here I don't dare touch you.'

Morna gave him an astounded look. Always before he'd removed her clothes in a lingering, erotic seduction. 'Why?'

He spread out his hands. 'Calluses,' he said simply, although his smile was pure male challenge. 'They'll ruin the material. So you'll have to take it off—slowly.'

A spurt of nervous laughter surprised her. Controlling it, she said, 'Only if I get to take your clothes off too.'

His eyes gleamed. 'My pleasure,' he said deeply. 'And that's no idle claim—it will be with my intense pleasure.'

If anyone had told Morna that she'd strip while a fully dressed man watched, she'd have laughed in their face. But now nothing seemed more right. While every thrumming cell responded to his complete attention, she took her time removing the slim golden dress.

Hawke's eyes narrowed into slits when he saw the fragile flesh-coloured undergarments beneath it.

'Leave the pendant on,' he said abrasively. 'It goes magnificently with your eyes.'

A velvet shiver danced down her spine. 'Fantasy time, Hawke?'

'It's not one I've had before,' he said, 'but knowing that you designed it and made it is—special.'

'No suspenders, I'm afraid,' she said with a slanting,

saucy grin as she stepped out of her shoes and began—slowly, carefully—to peel down the tights.

'Not a fantasy of mine.'

She looked up, and met eyes of burning emerald; a dark flush lay along his wide cheekbones, and his lips seemed a little fuller. Uncaged need roared through her, unforgiving, imperative.

The pendant fell forward when she eased the tights from her feet. Still holding his eyes, she removed her bra and the scrap of silk that was all that was left. Then, glorying in his locked stillness—as though he didn't dare move—she came up to him. 'Hold out your arms.'

A muscle flicked in his jaw, but he obeyed. 'Nice cufflinks,' she said, steadying her voice with difficulty as she deftly freed them from his sleeves. 'Excellent quality—made in England in the twenties or thirties, I'd say.'

'My great-grandfather's.'

A quick upward glance revealed the effort it took him to infuse his voice with that wry note of humour. He could do nothing to hide the primal undercurrents surging beneath his controlled surface.

'Of course,' she said lightly, loosening his tie and dropping it onto the floor.

He said, 'What's the matter?'

'Nothing.' She began on his studs.

It wasn't important that she'd never known a grandfather; she was enjoying her task too much to mull over old pain.

When the last stud had been released she pushed his shirt open to kiss the flesh beneath. His body sprang to life beneath her lips but he still didn't move, although his chest lifted sharply and she heard the beginning of a noise in his throat, a low, rough growl instantly stifled.

Soon, she thought recklessly, he'll lose that iron control totally—and enjoy it!

Eventually he was naked from the waist up, and a dangerous, palpable tension tightened between them.

Exulting in the heat and firmness of his skin beneath her fingers, the rapid thunder of his heart, she blocked out the knowledge that although sex meant little without respect and love and trust, this powerful hunger was still all they shared.

And because the thought hurt so much she took the final step towards him, and as his arms compelled her against his powerful, aroused body she yielded, pulling his dark head down to kiss his throat and the angular jut of his jaw.

'Morna,' he said almost angrily. 'I don't know how the hell you do this to me...'

'It's mutual.'

He looked down at her in his arms with the complex smile of a conqueror. 'I know,' he said simply, and carried her across to the bed, setting her on her feet only so that he could pull back the coverlet.

They kissed again, sinking onto the cool sheets until Hawke released her and sprawled back onto the pillows like a great cat, lithe and golden and utterly sure of himself.

Morna lifted herself on an elbow and looked her fill.

He laughed quietly. 'Like what you see?'

'You know I do,' she said with husky intentness.

'Then take it.' Green eyes gleaming, he paused before saying her name like a man who loved her.

CHAPTER ELEVEN

MORNA woke to the raucous cry of a gull, the salt tang of the sea, and a delicious indolence caused by too little sleep for the past two nights. Some time during the night Hawke had tried to wake her, but when she'd muttered and snuggled down again he'd laughed and kissed her and she'd been dragged into sleep's undertow again. Now she lay with her eyes closed, luxuriating in memories.

Last night she had taken Hawke, taken him with all the sensual finesse she could find in herself, replacing the lazy amusement in his eyes with an unsparing desire that stoked her own hunger. It had been wildly exciting—and intensely liberating—to make the moves, to treat his big body as her own territory, to do whatever she wanted with him and feel his helpless response.

He was the most confidently secure man she'd ever met and last night had showed her how skilled and experienced he was in the arts of love. Passion didn't come any better than that, she thought, aching with a complex mixture of emotions—happiness, a security she'd never aspired to, and a bleak foreboding.

In spite of her efforts to keep it simple and on the surface, she'd somehow tumbled into love with him. Quite literally, she realised with stark terror, she would die for him. He was tender and exciting and darkly compelling...

And he didn't love her. Oh, he wanted her, but now wanting wasn't enough for her.

Because that was their arrangement, she had to abide by it or leave him. And time with him was too precious to waste in regrets. So she wouldn't. Yawning, she groped across the bed, but her hand found only empty sheets.

She rolled over onto her back, wincing a little at the slight ache in her body, and opened heavy eyelids a slit. The curtains were still dark across the windows, although the probing morning sun had managed to penetrate the room with slivers of dancing golden light.

She listened, but apart from the low murmur of the sea a few metres away the house echoed with emptiness. Hawke must have gone across to the resort for some reason.

Yawning again, Morna moved over to his side of the bed, snuggling her face into the pillow to inhale the faint trace of male scent that belonged to him alone. She felt drugged, so lethargic she couldn't think. Drugged with pleasure...

When the shrill summons of the telephone sawed through her head she struggled up from sleep enough to automatically thrust out a hand. 'Hello,' she mumbled into the receiver.

'Could I speak to Hawke Challenger, please?'

She pushed hair back from her face, realising she should have left the answering machine to deal with the call. 'I'm afraid he's not here.'

'Well, can you tell him that Patrick Ward wants to speak to him?' When she said nothing, the caller went on, 'I'm back in New Zealand now. If he gives me a ring at this number we can finalise the agreement we came to in Singapore.' He paused. 'Got that?' he asked, a hint of impatience in his tone.

Numbly, Morna grabbed the pen by the telephone. 'Yes.'

'Then take down this number, please.' He had to go

through it twice because Morna's sluggish brain had stopped when he'd said his name.

'Right, thanks,' he said, and hung up.

Stiff as a robot, Morna got out of bed and stood for a long moment staring down at the tangled sheets as the conversation tumbled in jagged segments around her brain.

Patrick Ward. Jacob Ward's son. The agreement we came to in Singapore.

'So he's alive,' she said stupidly, rubbing a shaking hand across her eyes. 'Poor Jacob...'

Jacob had mourned his son, accepting his death although no body had ever been found. If only he'd known that Patrick was alive.

Shaking her head, Morna blinked back stinging tears. She had to *think*.

Somehow Hawke had found Patrick Ward, and instead of telling her he'd gone behind her back and made a pre-emptive move.

Stomach clenching, she looked down at her naked body, the body he'd taken such pleasure from the previous night. Her arms came up to fold protectively over her breasts and shield her heart.

When had he found out that Patrick Ward was still alive? Nausea made her swallow several times as the bits of information slotted together into a hideous jigsaw.

Had Hawke lied right from the beginning? Painfully she recalled his barely concealed dislike of her after they'd met. Of course he'd noticed that she was attracted to him—he knew women well.

Morna forced herself to ignore the anguish slicing through her and face what facts she knew. Had he deliberately set out to seduce her into selling him the bach and its precious three acres of land? If so, she'd aided in her own seduction. Hooked by her mindless response to his particular brand of magnetism, she'd chosen not to listen to the little voice that warned her no man could be trusted.

Raw humiliation acrid in her mouth, she wondered if eventually she'd have surrendered and sold him the property instead of donating it to charity.

'No,' she said aloud.

But she'd just admitted that she'd die for him.

'Not now,' she said, the words icy fragments of pain in the silent room. She shivered.

Once he'd realised that he couldn't manipulate her with sex he'd have rejected her, just like Glen.

Another shaft of pain speared her with an agony so intense she crumpled onto the side of the bed. This was all speculation. But it made sense—because Patrick Ward wasn't speculation, and neither was the deal he'd made with Hawke in Singapore.

'*Think*, you idiot,' she said with gritty desperation. 'Forget about whether or not you'd have sold Tarika Bay to him—it's not important now.'

What was important was that he'd found Patrick Ward and without telling her had come to an agreement with the man, when he knew—surely he knew?—she'd see it as a betrayal.

Only a man who didn't care about their relationship could have done that.

A low, keening noise escaped her as she hid her face in her hands. She despised Hawke for his cynical exploitation and his lies of omission, but this debacle was her fault. Made mindless by passion, she'd wilfully, stupidly, *deliberately* forgotten every bitter lesson she'd learned from the past.

Blinking back unshed tears, she lifted her head and noted the golden dress on the chair and her tights in a filmy heap, her underclothes in another where she'd dropped them in that sleazy striptease the previous night.

She had to get out of here before he found her.

In the bathroom she found a large folded towel on the counter that Hawke must have left for her; beside it was her evening bag, along with a pair of her jeans and a shirt, and her sneakers.

He must have gone to the bach and collected them.

Then she saw the note.

It was the first time she'd seen his writing; her heart cramped, but she read it swiftly.

Darling, I've been called away—one of my managers in the South Island has been badly hurt. I might not be able to get in touch, but I'll ring you tonight if I can. I hope you slept well.

Signed with his initial. Although her eyes fixed hungrily on the salutation, his consideration wounded her.

'Hypocrite!' she said fiercely. He was probably in Auckland, contacting Patrick Ward.

She bit her lip hard enough to break the delicate skin and showered and changed before stripping the sheets, dumping them into the laundry basket and remaking the bed. The betraying scrap of paper with the telephone number and message went on top of Hawke's note with its lying salutation.

Then she picked up the clothes she'd discarded the previous night and walked out of the house and over the hill—out of his life, away from the love she'd resisted so strongly that she hadn't acknowledged its existence until she'd discovered it was based on lies.

* * *

Annie hurtled into the workroom. 'He's back.'

'I don't want to see him,' Morna said, her remote voice at odds with her constricted breathing. She measured the height of the rounded cabochon emerald with a pair of dividers, then put the stone down. You want to know the length of this bezel, she told herself. So measure it.

But her hands were shaking.

Annie still hovered. 'Ah—he looks as though what you want isn't of much concern to him,' she said carefully.

'Just tell him to go. And next time don't let him into the shop.'

'Why don't you tell me yourself?' Hawke's voice, cold and deadly.

Morna ran the dividers along the surface of the gold strip and wrote down the figures. Only then did she turn. Hawke stood, big and dark and dominant, in the doorway, his face set in cold, intimidating lines.

She said in her most frigid voice, 'This is a secure area.'

'All the better.'

He looked at Annie, who glanced worriedly from one to the other. 'Any shouting and I'll call the police,' she said firmly before leaving.

'Now,' Hawke said, still in that flat, lethal tone, 'perhaps you'll tell me why you moved out of the bach?'

Head held high, Morna got to her feet and faced him. She wasn't going to let him dominate her in her own workroom. 'Because I no longer wanted to live there,' she said, her tone matching his.

'So where are you living?' He was watching her closely, his eyes unyielding as ice.

'That is none of your business.' Morna lifted her chin, trying to armour herself against his formidable presence.

Let him get this off his chest and go, because she was dying of anguish.

'Why did you run away?'

'I'm sure you've already worked that out,' she sneered.

'Because you're a coward,' he said softly, pale eyes opaque and uncompromising. 'Why didn't you stay and face me after Patrick Ward told you I was negotiating to buy Tarika Bay?'

'Why should I?' The words were acrid in her mouth. 'What else was there to learn?'

'You could have asked me what the hell I was up to.'

'I know what you were up to. You want to buy Tarika Bay from him once he gets it,' she said, and waited with humiliating hope for a reason she could accept.

She didn't get it. After a short pause Hawke said deliberately, 'You and he would have quite a lot in common—he's as fascinated by the allure of gems as you are.'

'I know,' she said stonily while hope died a bitter death. 'Jacob told me about him.'

'He was taken prisoner and rotted in some equatorial gaol for three years, suffering God knows what privations, before he finally escaped. Once he got out he wrote to his father. The letter was forwarded on to Jacob's executor, who contacted me.'

'When?' She held her breath.

He paused, then said levelly, 'Three days before I went to Singapore to meet him.'

It was confirmation of all her suspicions. 'So you saw your chance and took it,' she said tonelessly. 'Naturally you wouldn't tell me, but why didn't the executor get onto my solicitor?'

He surveyed her with an analytical lack of emotion that cracked the brittle shield of her anger. 'Because he thought you were a common, greedy little trollop who'd looked at an old, vulnerable, dying man and seen an opportunity to make some easy money.'

Although she flinched, her proud white face showed no emotion. 'So he tarred and feathered me without a shred of proof.'

'It's common knowledge that Glen Spencer supported you for years, and that when you left him you took a golden handshake. It's also generally accepted that you and Nick Harding were lovers,' Hawke said coolly.

'And you believed that?' Her voice rang with disdain.

'Not Nick.' He examined her face with ruthless objectivity. 'As soon as I saw you two together I knew there was nothing—never had been anything—between you.'

So badly wounded she had to formulate each word separately, she said harshly, 'Very perceptive of you. As for Glen, I'm still paying back his money. I was fond of Jacob, but I asked him not to leave me the bach, and if I'd known about his son I wouldn't have accepted it. You didn't really have to go to all the trouble of sleeping with me to get your hands on it.'

'Is that all it was for you—an affair?'

The slashing contempt in his words made her quail internally, but anger held her upright—anger, and a stubborn refusal to let him see how much his duplicity hurt her.

She shrugged. 'Probably an affair needs to last a little longer, have more emotion mixed up in it. Call it an extended one-night stand,' she said indifferently. 'You thought you could seduce the property from me, and fortunately for your plans I wanted you. Not that it would have worked—I'd still have given it to the Kids at the Beach charity.' She met the dark fury of his gaze with uncompromising, stubborn defiance. 'But that doesn't matter any more. And you've got what you want so there's no need to pretend any longer.'

'Have you got what you want?' he asked deliberately, letting his hard gaze drift over her face and breasts.

Her treacherous body leapt helplessly into full-blown life. Shamed and angry, she counter-attacked, dredging up the energy to say with aloof and delicate scorn, 'Oh, we'd probably have lasted until I found out you'd gone behind my back—you're brilliant in bed. But like most people I turn surly when I find I've been manipulated. Now get out of my life.'

He hesitated, then said in a different voice, 'Morna, listen—'

Her heart splintered. Before he could produce excuses for his behaviour she said scathingly, 'Tarika Bay is now legally Patrick Ward's. I signed over all claim to it this morning.' She looked at him with empty eyes. 'So you've won, Hawke. I hope it's worth what you paid for it. And now, if you don't mind, I have work to do.'

Hawke turned on his heel and left.

Sometime in the future she'd be glad she'd cut him off, because if she'd listened to him she might have let herself trust him again.

But nothing had ever hurt so much. Glen's betrayal had been painful, but this—this was a piercing agony. Yet she'd had no illusions about Hawke!

From the door Annie said stoutly, 'No man's worth it.'

Morna looked up. 'I know that.' Her voice was husky and strained, but she managed a brief grimace that might have passed for a smile in the dark.

'Do you want me to ring someone?'

'No.'

Nick had been her saviour when Glen dumped her—in

spite of being exiled half a world away, she'd clung desperately to his support—but now Nick had Cathy.

Anyway, she'd grown up since then. She'd cope. Picking up the dividers, she stared blindly down at the gold sheet. 'I'll be fine,' she said, without looking at Annie.

'Trust me, it doesn't last,' Annie said firmly. 'I don't think of that sleazeball I married at all now.'

The insistent summons of the doorbell interrupted her. 'Oh, all right,' she muttered, and after a worried glance left the workroom.

Morna closed her eyes for a second. 'Pull yourself together,' she said almost soundlessly. 'It's over and you've got no one but yourself to blame. Now you've got to remember the lesson and forget the man. And work is the simplest way to do that.'

Work helped, of course. So did a call from the police a week later to tell her they'd caught the ram-raiders, although the jewels they'd stolen had long vanished.

From then on each perusal of the amount she owed the bank was enough to keep her slogging on into the night, trying to make up the time she'd wasted with Hawke. And things began to go well for her.

The engaged couple finally made up their minds, so she had their rings to craft, and the bride's mother's wedding tiara to refurbish. She was also commissioned to design a necklace of opals and diamonds for the spoiled young wife of a middle-aged industrialist.

A cruise ship brought in several tourists who had seen her display on board; they bought from the shop, and two of them commissioned designs that were flashing back and forth on the fax machine.

So, professionally, things were improving fast. It might have been because she'd donated that pendant to the charity ball and caught the right eyes; more likely, she thought cynically, going to the ball with Hawke had bestowed on her some invisible cachet of approval.

Perhaps her new popularity was a morsel of sympathy, a kind of second prize from fate.

Yet each night when she arrived exhausted back at the poky room she was renting she couldn't sleep; instead she spent hours going over and over in obsessive detail the time she'd spent with Hawke.

Annie began to cluck about the weight she was losing, even arriving at the shop with delicious treats she'd cooked. To please her Morna forced them past the lump in her throat, but she couldn't hide the haunted bleakness of her eyes, or the shadows beneath them. So her assistant started bringing in herbal concoctions that promised a natural night's sleep. Obediently Morna tried them, until eventually exhaustion worked its own cure and she began sleeping heavily, waking unrefreshed and dull-eyed each morning.

Cathy and Nick worried about her, but she refused to sully their happiness with her misery. Her smile might be mechanical and too bright, but it was frequent, even when gossip columnists began to hint that a certain gorgeous pastoralist and a lovely Auckland woman were appearing together everywhere. After reading the first coy allusion in stone-faced anguish, Morna refused to read any more.

'Mrs Roberton's in again,' Annie announced, showing her teeth as she kept an eye on the customer in the shop monitor. 'She wants you to design a brooch for her. She didn't say anything about the ring she had you make, which she then turned down.'

'Tell her I don't have the time,' Morna said with cynical satisfaction. Repaying the bank loan was important, but sometimes all a woman could hold on to was her pride.

'I will certainly do that.' Annie smiled vengefully.

'It's the truth, anyway. I've got to get things done for this exhibition.'

That was another good thing. She'd been invited to exhibit at a very prestigious Australian occasion. She just wished she felt some enthusiasm for such an excellent chance to widen her clientele.

'I'm so going to enjoy seeing her expression when I tell her the only thing you'd design for her would be coffin plates,' Annie said cheerfully.

'You wouldn't!'

'Well, no, but it's a huge temptation.' Fixing a charming smile onto her face, Annie went out.

Morna got up and walked across the room, pushing a hand into the small of her back. She tore a leaf off the calendar; almost three months since she'd listened to Jacob Ward's son kill her happiness.

In spite of her own experience—and Annie's assurance that such grief couldn't last—it hadn't faded. She railed at herself for being so stupid, for falling in love with a man who'd promised her nothing at all but fantastic sex...

'He certainly delivered on that,' she said aloud, riffling through the mail.

Get a grip, she advised herself ruthlessly. You'll cope, because you have to.

A fat registered letter from a firm of solicitors hollowed out her stomach. 'Smytheman and Force,' she muttered. 'What on earth—? Oh.'

The firm who'd dealt with Jacob's estate. She ripped it open, braced for a cold summary from the executor of the winding up of the estate.

'That settled her hash, Friday-faced old harridan,' Annie said with gleeful satisfaction, gliding into the room. 'She didn't believe me, of course, when I said you were too busy, but she couldn't say anything. She— Morna! *What's the matter?'*

White-faced, Morna lifted her head. 'Deeds,' she said vaguely.

'Deeds?' Annie's gaze fell onto the papers in her employer's hands. 'What sort of deeds?'

Morna gripped the back of a chair. 'Property deeds.'

Annie had no idea what was going on, but she was a practical woman who'd endured more than her share of trauma. 'You need a stiff drink, but a cup of coffee will have to do,' she said. 'Sit down and I'll make it.'

But Morna remained standing while she read the letter again. In stiff legalese, every word frozen with disapproval, the solicitor informed her that, acting in accordance with the instructions of Mr Hawke Challenger, he was enclosing the documents that gave her possession of such and such a parcel of land marked on the enclosed map.

Tarika Bay.

'Why?' she whispered, squelching a wildly burgeoning hope. *'Why?'*

A belated attack of conscience? 'Not likely,' she scoffed. And even if it was she didn't want Hawke feeling sorry for her.

She put the envelope and the deeds on the table and at last collapsed into the chair. No, she wanted him hungry for her, wildly, passionately in love with her, obsessing about her as much as she longed for him—

'Oh, grow up,' she said rigidly.

'I am grown up.' Annie plonked a cup of coffee in front of her. 'Not that you should be drinking coffee, because you're already wired, but if you won't touch herbal teas you'll have to make do with this.' She glanced over her shoulder as the doorbell chimed discreetly. 'Morna, drink it down, *please*. You're as white as a sheet.'

Morna curved her hands around the mug of pale coffee, sipped, and almost gagged. Annie must have tipped half the sugarbowl into it.

She'd nag if it wasn't drunk, so Morna stoically downed the disgusting stuff, staring at the deeds as though they'd been soaked in contact poison.

What was she going to do?

Eventually she rang her own solicitor. 'Can anyone give me land?' she asked abruptly.

His cough made her drag in a juddering breath and start again. 'Sorry, that's not what I meant. Can a parcel of land be made legally mine without me signing anything?'

'For it to be legally yours,' he said, clearly shocked by the idea, 'you would have to sign various documents, of course.'

'I thought so,' she said. 'Thank you.'

'Do you want to make an appointment?'

'That won't be necessary,' she told him through gritted teeth, and hung up, a woman transformed. After three months of wretched lethargy a rush of furious energy filled her.

'Hawke Challenger,' she announced to the empty room as she scooped up the deeds and stuffed them into her briefcase, 'is going to have his *gift* flung back in his face. See how he likes that!'

But she'd keep it businesslike. So she wasn't going anywhere near his resort at Somerville's Bay—and not even to herself did she admit that she couldn't bear to recall that last night with him, the ecstasy and then the betrayal.

No, she'd go to his office. And she wouldn't ring and forewarn him either—she'd take a chance on him being there. If he wasn't, she'd simply dump the deeds on his assistant and leave. But if he was...

She smiled evilly. If he *was* there, she decided, slamming the door of her new old wreck of a car, she'd let him know exactly what she thought of men who assumed she could be bought off. He couldn't have chosen a more humiliating, aggressive way to make her angry.

When she reached Orewa, a holiday town sprawling the length of its exquisite beach, she parked along the street from his office. Anticipation quivered in her stomach, and for the first time since she'd heard Patrick Ward's voice on the telephone she felt alive again—too alive, in fact. Peering in the mirror to refresh her lipstick and comb her hair, she realised she looked positively scary, her glittering eyes and the hectic flush along her cheekbones enough to frighten children.

Amazing what adrenalin could do!

Hawke's office was in a block a little off the main street; in the lobby Morna noted the signs for a dentist, a doctor and a lawyer among others.

She worked off some of her nervous energy by striding up the stairs. At the top she glanced along a hallway redeemed from bland neutrality by judiciously placed plants and pictures.

And there was the sign for Challenger Holdings. Blood drumming an urgent tattoo throughout her body, she opened the door into a pleasant reception room presided over by a small, middle-aged woman with violently red hair. Another door led to what was presumably Hawke's office.

At Morna's entrance the red-headed woman looked up and smiled. 'Can I help you?'

'I'd like to see Mr Challenger,' Morna said, her mouth as dry as her tone.

'Is he expecting you?'

'I'm sure he is,' Morna told her with a steely smile.

CHAPTER TWELVE

THE receptionist's hand hovered over a telephone. 'Ah—who shall I say it is?'

'Morna Vause.'

'Certainly, Ms Vause.' The woman punched in a number and said, 'Hawke, Ms Vause is here to see you.' She put the receiver down and eyed Morna with stringently restrained interest. 'He'll be here in a moment.'

The sound of the door opening made Morna's heart lurch and dissipated the burst of energy that had sustained her so far. Turning, she thought despairingly, *This is a huge mistake,* but her gaze fixed hungrily on the man who came through the door.

Hawke looked tired. Not exhausted, but the fabulous face seemed slightly older, a little more lean, and the splendid vitality had dimmed. However, the gleam in the green eyes was just the same, and the smile that curled his beautiful mouth sent her heart-rate bolting into the stratosphere.

'Hello, Morna.' He sounded as though he'd been expecting her. 'Come into my office.' Without taking his eyes off her, he said, 'Barbara, bring in some coffee, please. And biscuits.'

His office was big and airy, its windows opening onto a view of the bay. 'Sit down,' he suggested with a bland courtesy that set Morna's teeth on edge, before adding abrasively, 'What the hell have you been doing to yourself?'

She stayed erect, whipping up her anger to white heat.

'Nothing,' she returned. Her voice sounded creaky and thin, as though she hadn't spoken for years. She groped in her briefcase and pulled out the deeds to the bach.

'I have no idea why you did this,' she said, dropping them on the desk, 'but I don't want Tarika Bay.'

She should have stopped there. Instead, she glanced at his shuttered face and went on with barely caged passion, 'And I intensely resent the fact that you thought I'd accept conscience money from you.'

He ignored the deeds. 'I asked you a question. What the hell have you been doing to yourself?'

'I don't know what you mean,' she said haughtily, spun off balance.

'You look like something left out and forgotten over the winter,' he said brutally, strolling up to her and taking her chin in his hand. 'You're pale, you've got dark circles under your eyes, and you've lost weight.'

Morna clamped her eyes shut, unable to meet the intent probe of his. 'Let me go,' she snapped. It sounded childish, but her brain was running on instinct alone.

He didn't move. 'Have you been ill?'

Sick with love, she thought viciously. Mad too. 'No, just busy. I've been working hard.'

Although he let her go then, it was with a lifted brow and a silent, uncompromising invitation to continue.

She forced her lips into a thin, artificial smile and had to unlock her jaw to say, 'I don't want Tarika Bay. Don't try to send the deeds to me again because I'll courier them back.'

'Why didn't you do that this time?' he asked, his idle tone at variance with his flinty green eyes.

Good question. Morna opened her mouth to answer, and realised she didn't have one. Or rather, the truthful answer—that she'd craved to see him again—was the one pride absolutely forbade.

'Why did you send me the deeds?' she parried, mind scurrying because she was losing her grip on the conversation.

'Answering one question with another is the last resort of someone with nowhere to go,' he told her ruthlessly. 'I wanted to see you again without being interrupted by your watchdog of an assistant, and I knew you'd never agree to a meeting.'

The surge of joy at his admission had faded by the time he'd finished speaking. 'How did you know I wouldn't accept the land?' Her lips curled at his shrug. 'You were taking a risk. A woman who'd target an old man on the off-chance he'd leave her his property wouldn't think twice about accepting a valuable piece of land from a past lover.'

'I'm not averse to the occasional risk,' he said enigmatically, and before she had time to call him on this rudeness he went on, 'But in this case I was pretty sure. However, I had a contingency plan; if you'd posted them back I'd decided to kidnap you.'

Her jaw dropped. No expression showed in his boldly chiselled features and his eyes were opaque, but she suspected that he meant exactly what he'd said. Bewildered, she demanded, 'What is this all about?'

'Tell me why you brought those deeds up here instead of stuffing them into the first courier bag that came your way and sending them back.'

She chewed her lip. 'I was—*am*,' she corrected hastily, 'furious. I wanted to tell you what I thought of you.'

His cynical smile made him seem older. 'So what are you waiting for?'

But she shook her head and walked away from him to

stand in front of the window. A peacock sea glimmered through the symmetrical pyramids of Norfolk Island pines along the beach. As she stared out an elderly man strolling along the beach leaned over and kissed the woman beside him. Morna's throat clogged with unshed tears.

'Why did you want to see me?' she asked harshly, a terrible hope flowering inside her.

'I heard that the police had tracked down the ram-raiders.'

Startled, she looked over her shoulder. 'Yes.'

'Did any of the stolen stock turn up?'

'No.'

'So how are things going for you? Apart from your health, of course,' he said smoothly.

'There's nothing wrong with my health,' she retorted. 'I've just been working.'

'Working yourself to death, by the look of it.'

What on earth was going on here? She sent him a blank look, colouring when she caught him examining her in a cool, unsparing assessment. She said uncertainly, 'Hawke, why did you want to see me?'

When he didn't answer straight away she turned to face him across the room. He said dispassionately, 'I wanted to make sure you're all right.'

The tiny, merciless flicker of hope began to build inside her foolish heart. Trying to quench it, she said formally, 'I'm fine, thank you. I've been busy with a lot of commissions.'

Keeping his eyes fixed on her face, he leaned back onto his desk, folded his arms and said with silky clarity, 'You kept remarkably silent about large chunks of your life. You didn't tell me you had to repay the clients whose pieces were stolen from your safe.'

She opened her mouth to deny it, then closed it again.

It would be no use—he knew. 'Who said that? Nick? Or Cathy—'

'Neither Nick nor Cathy,' he interrupted smoothly. 'You have loyal friends.'

The door opened and his receptionist came in with a tray. She set it down on the desk, smiled at them both and said, 'Chocolate biscuits.'

'Thanks, Barbara.' Hawke waited until the door had closed behind her before indicating the tray. 'Pour yourself some coffee. You look as though you could do with sustenance.'

Morna hesitated, but poured two cups, handing him the one without milk before taking hers and lifting it to shelter behind its flimsy protection.

After a couple of fortifying mouthfuls she asked abruptly, 'How did you know I'd taken a loss with that raid?'

'I saw that the safe hadn't been forced, so I assumed it had been left unsecured.' He waited for her reluctant nod before resuming. 'And I knew Babs Pickersgill's pearls were in it—that night at the pearl show she'd told me you were restringing them for her. It didn't seem likely that your insurance company would have paid out on the contents of an unsecured safe, and I guessed that Babs's necklace wasn't the only client's piece there.'

'There were others,' she admitted, a tendril of fear winding its way down her backbone.

Watching her closely, he said, 'Why didn't you tell me?'

'Why should I? It had nothing to do with you.' She wished she knew what was going on in the sharp, brilliant brain behind his narrowed eyes. To forestall any further probing, she went on, 'I got a loan from the bank. You don't have to worry about me, Hawke, if that's your problem. I'm a survivor.'

'It's something we have in common,' he said, still watching her with that unnerving green gaze, penetrating as a laser. He looked as though he was determined to drill the truth out of her. 'We have quite a lot in common. Lack of trust, for example.'

Morna bit her lip.

Without giving her time to answer, he went on, 'We spent almost a month in each other's beds, but I still know very little about you. You were everything a man could ask, in bed and out, but I hadn't been your lover for long before I started to wonder why you kept yourself hidden behind that shiny, seamless mask. You had no intention of making the relationship anything more than sexual.'

'Just as well,' she flashed, sick with humiliation. 'I could have been very badly hurt if I'd learned to trust you. No one likes being used.'

'Is that what you thought I was doing—using you?' His coldly incredulous voice brought shamed colour to her cheeks. 'For the record,' he said between his teeth, 'I am not into sexual exploitation—any sort of exploitation.'

Her colour deepened. The rationale she had used to go to bed with him seemed tawdry and cheap now. Wishing she'd never given in to the desire to see him again, she said roughly, 'Neither am I.'

Only at first—and even then she'd been in love with him. She must have fallen in love with him at the Agricultural Show—she just hadn't admitted it, not even to herself.

He returned judicially, 'I know that now.'

She flared with raw passion, 'Did you really think I made a habit of seducing men so I could extract money from them?'

'When I first met you I wasn't sure. You had a certain reputation,' he responded with deliberate calmness. 'You lived with Glen Spencer for five years. When he decided it was over he paid for your studies overseas.'

'I repaid every cent.' She bared her teeth at him, adding scornfully, 'Not that I'll be able to prove it.'

Hawke's black brows drew together. 'It's none of my business what you did with the money.'

'But you believed the gossip.'

He shook his head. 'I had an open mind.'

'Well, listen to the truth. Yes, Glen paid me off with the design course to get me out of the way. He hated being made to look mean, even to himself, so when I treated it as a loan he left it to me in his will.' She paused, then said, 'He had cancer.'

'I see,' Hawke said quietly, his expression closed and forbidding.

'So I used that yo-yoing money to finance myself into the shop, but it's still a loan as far as I'm concerned, so I'm paying it back to charity,' Morna said fiercely. 'I'll finish doing that as soon as I've repaid the bank loan.'

'I think I'm beginning to understand.' Hawke's voice was cool and dispassionate.

Recklessly, hands clenched at her sides and her voice crisp, she added, 'I couldn't live with myself if I didn't get rid of it—it's a burden to me.' She shot him a fiery glance, glittering and golden and defiant. 'And, no, I can't—*won't*—prove that, either. I won't show you the receipts.'

No emotions showed in his cold, handsome face. 'You don't have to prove it. I believe you.' Before she'd had time to digest this he said, 'But is it so surprising that I wondered how you'd come to be left Tarika Bay?'

'If you were interested why didn't you ask me?'

He set his coffee cup down. 'I did. You made it obvious you weren't going to discuss any more than the bare bones. And I soon found that that proviso extended to every other part of your life.'

'I told you about my childhood,' she muttered.

'In a couple of bitter sentences. And not once in the entire time that we were sleeping together did you ask about mine. So I assumed that your interest in me stopped outside the sheets.' His voice was even, but there was no mistaking the contempt in it.

Ashamed, Morna turned her head away. She'd been so determined to shore up her defences and make sure she didn't let herself get close to him, because if she didn't know him she couldn't learn to need him...

'You were wrong,' she said defensively, wondering why she was telling him this. 'We were just—we didn't have the sort of relationship that relies on exchanged confidences.'

'You made sure of that.' His voice was level, yet she saw something very like pain flicker in his eyes.

It had never occurred to her he might want more than sex. That persistent hope unfurled inside her. 'Why didn't you tell me Patrick Ward had been found? You must have known how I'd feel about what you did.'

After a short pause he said briefly, 'I was scared.'

Her head jerked up and she was startled into a laugh of disbelief. 'You?'

'You'd said nothing about how you felt.' His smile was hard with inwardly directed derision, his eyes metallic.

'You must have known how I felt—you *did* know!' she retorted indignantly.

'I knew you wanted me.' He paused, then added, 'What scared me was that I craved more than that.'

Morna struggled to repress that remorseless, surging

hope. She said coldly, 'So did I pass some kind of test by refusing Tarika Bay? Did that convince you I don't go out trawling for elderly men who might leave me legacies?'

He said between his teeth, 'I did not test you. By then I'd realised that I'd let myself be sidetracked by stale, malicious rumours. Unfortunately, when you told me you'd renounced your claim to Jacob Ward's estate, you also told me to get out of your life.'

'What did you expect?'

He shrugged. 'I suppose I expected some trust.'

'Really?' she asked, fighting down a weak-kneed urge to tell him it didn't matter, she loved him and she was prepared to forgive him anything. 'But you did go behind my back. What other construction could I have put on it?'

'Did I ever tell you that I took Babs Pickersgill out to dinner after the pearl showing?'

Startled by the abrupt change of subject, Morna shook her head. So much for the miserable hours she'd spent imagining him in Peri's arms! But what had Babs, with her kind heart and gossiping tendencies—?

Gossip! 'What did she tell you?' she asked thinly.

'That Glen Spencer stopped you working when you lived with him. She also intimated that although people thought you'd played on his guilty conscience to extract money from him, she knew better.' Hawke's smile was brief and unamused.

'She's on the board of the charity I pay Glen's legacy to,' Morna said, shaken and defensive.

He nodded. 'And she told me that you buy your clothes in secondhand shops.'

Morna flushed scarlet and kept her eyes fixed on the people passing in the street below. 'She had no right,' she muttered.

Hawke said quietly, 'She knew I was fascinated by you, and she likes you. I think she fancied herself as a match-maker.'

Shock battered her in a monstrous, overwhelming wave. Fists clenched at her sides, she couldn't trust her voice enough to speak.

He said thoughtfully, 'Tarika Bay is yours, so swallow your stiff-necked pride and accept it. By the way, it's not suitable for a children's camp; there's a beach on the other side of the peninsula that will be much safer. I've organ-ised for it to be subdivided off.'

In a muted, dangerous voice Morna demanded, 'Why do you want me to have it?'

'When I drove home after we made love the first time I stopped at the top of the hill and asked myself what the hell I'd got into. I'd thought that making love to you would ease the grip you had on me, but I knew then that I was never going to be able to prise you out of my mind.' He paused and said lethally, 'I don't like to admit it, but it made me angry. I intensely disliked the idea of being beholden to anyone for my happiness.'

His happiness? Not a word of love. Yet Morna's heart jumped into her throat. Deep inside something snapped and pain shot through her, so intense she could barely breathe.

'Why?' she asked.

'Because it had never happened to me before,' he said with devastating simplicity. 'So after we made love I stayed away for as long as I could. Two whole days! I despised myself all over again for not being able to resist you; it gave you power over me. But for the first time in my life I couldn't keep my distance. And so we became lovers.'

Not a muscle moved in his big body, or his lean, handsome face. Tension smoked between them, chaining Morna in place as she listened.

Still in that even, judicious tone, he went on, 'Right from the start I wanted to help you.'

Morna went white, her eyes dilating as she stared at him. She wasn't, she thought numbly, surprised. She'd always sensed a protective streak in him a mile wide.

When she didn't speak he went on, 'In the month we were together I realised—far too slowly, because I fought it all the way—that you were not greedy or conniving. But I still demanded proof. And I wanted you to admit that you felt more for me than a sexual need. When you gave me the proof of your honesty—when you told me you'd signed over Tarika Bay to Patrick Ward—you also showed me that you would never be able to trust me. And that was when I found out what pain really is.'

Eyes huge with surprise, Morna swallowed to ease her parched throat, but the voice that emerged was croaky and hoarse. 'Why did you contact Patrick Ward?'

He gave a humourless smile. 'Because by then I knew that you wouldn't accept help from me, and that as soon as he turned up you'd hand the Bay back to him. I wanted to give you Tarika Bay. Once I came back from Singapore I knew I'd have to tell you what I'd done. But first I wanted to bind you to me, and the only way I knew to do it was through sex.'

'So after you came back—?'

'Yes. I was trying to make you mine in every way that mattered, so that when I told you what I'd agreed with Patrick Ward you'd forgive me. Our last night together, when that idiot of a manager of mine hurt himself in the South Island, I'd planned to do it the next morning. Even when the call came through I tried to wake you and tell you then.'

'I wish you had,' she said sadly, remembering the distant recollection of him calling her name and her inability to respond.

He nodded, his expression sombre. 'I didn't because you were so exhausted you hadn't even stirred when the phone rang. It never occurred to me that Patrick Ward would ring. And when I came back it was to find you'd run away, and I'd effectively ruined any way of making you believe me. Hoist with my own petard I believe is the colloquial term for it.'

Swivelling back to face the window, Morna looked out over the pleasant bustle of the street below, the ordinary, everyday familiarity of life in small-town New Zealand, set in transcendent beauty so familiar it was taken for granted.

In a level, bleak voice Hawke said, 'Jacob Ward's will has been probated, and I closed the deal yesterday.' His smile was humourless. 'You see, I knew you wouldn't accept money from me—you're almost pathologically determined not to accept money from any man, aren't you?'

And when she didn't answer he asked, 'Has it occurred to you that by returning every cent Glen Spencer gave you you're punishing yourself for falling in love with him?'

'I feel—I felt that it was tainted,' she said, so low she wondered if he could hear her. 'That as long as I hadn't paid it all back I was tainted too.'

'Nothing could taint you,' he said, his voice much closer to her than it had been.

If only he'd touch her—but he wouldn't sweep her off her feet. That wasn't his style. He wouldn't use the easy, honeyed oblivion of sex to persuade her—he wanted complete surrender. Light-headed, as though she'd forgotten to inhale, she dragged in a deep, jarring breath. The bright sun dazzled her eyes and she couldn't hear the traffic for the wild hammering of her heart.

Hawke said, 'I banked on you storming up here to fling the deeds in my face. And I was right—you did come. Is it too late for us, Morna?'

She said hoarsely, 'You've been going out with Peri Carrington.'

'She's about to announce her engagement to a high country station owner in the South Island—a cousin of mine.'

Morna stood silent, so desperate to believe him that she knew she was lost.

He said, 'Did it hurt to hear that we'd been seen together?'

She clenched her hands on the windowsill, watching as the knuckles turned white. If she told him the truth now she was giving him the surrender he wanted. She'd vowed never to love again, never to give her heart into any man's careless keeping.

But if she didn't she would regret it for the rest of her life.

She swallowed and whispered, 'Yes.'

He said gravely, 'I'm sorry I dealt with Patrick Ward behind your back. Can you trust me never to do anything like that again?' And when she didn't answer, he said, 'You trusted Annie not to leave the safe unsecured again after the ram-raid. If you can trust her, then surely you can trust me?'

She was melting, the icily stiff pride that had protected her turning into torrents and carrying her with it down the mountain and into a warm spring countryside. Swinging clumsily around, she looked up into his beloved face and said, 'Hawke, I don't know what to do.'

'Love me,' he said instantly, his voice tender and uncompromising. 'I think you could if you tried. Because I love you more than I love life itself. I looked at you and loved you even before I knew you, and if I'd had any sense I'd have handed you my heart that day at the show and asked you to marry me then, instead of putting us both through hell.'

Morna's eyes filled with tears; the incredible had really happened. 'I don't have to learn to love you,' she said raggedly. 'I love you so much I think I might die from it. At first—yes, I thought I could have a passionate affair without losing my heart. But I should have known I was just looking for a way to save face. Loving is so dangerous.'

'Yes, but the rewards are so great,' he said with a calm conviction that finally convinced her, and he took her into his arms and kissed her.

She responded with an alacrity that had him tighten his arms around her and kiss her again, until a prolonged toot from the street lifted his head.

From the opposite footpath a raucous male voice yelled out, 'Way to go, mate!'

Half a second later this was seconded by a female voice. 'And matess!'

Laughing, Hawke waved to the onlookers and pulled Morna back so she could no longer be seen from the street. She laughed too, glorying in the change in his face—that indefinable air of strain was gone, the control snapped by happiness and love.

'I'll never be able to hold up my head again in this town,' he said, and suddenly his amusement died, and he said quietly, 'Morna. Beloved. I don't know when I realised that every time I said your name I was calling you Beloved in my heart.'

Morna gulped. 'I'm going to cry.'

'Darling heart, you can cry if you want to.'

But, although she kept her face hidden in his shoulder, she fought back the tears. Held safely against the warmth of his body, that indefinable scent that was Hawke filling her mind with hazy desire, she luxuriated in an unexpected, wonderful sense of security.

Eventually he said, 'Come out of there.'

She lifted a flushed face and smiled at him. 'I love you,' she said, giving him the most wonderful gift in the world. 'I'll always love you. I didn't know it could be like this.'

'Neither did I,' he said, eyes clear and warm, his beautiful mouth curving. 'When are we getting married?'

'Married?'

He smiled. 'It seems the natural thing to do—unless you have a decided objection to it? I suspect that Nick wouldn't like it if you just moved in with me.'

Morna blurted, 'You're younger than I am.'

His brows shot up. 'Two years?'

'It sounds silly to worry about it,' she admitted, feeling foolish.

'So don't. Not now, not ever again.' He looked down into her face and smiled wryly. 'Unless you make an honest man of me you can expect to sustain a visit from my mother. She's formidable enough on her own, but if you prove recalcitrant she'll probably call in reinforcements.'

'What sort?' She was dazzled at the idea of a family.

'About a hundred cousins, all very opinionated and bossy. I wouldn't blame you if you decided to cut and run, but they're a fact of my life.'

Morna said bleakly, 'Your mother is probably going to think you've lost your mind. I've got no family. I don't even know who my father was.'

'My mother will love you,' he said with a complete confidence she envied. 'And the fact that you're two years older than I am will encourage her to start dropping heavy hints about ageing eggs and how good it will be to start a family immediately. My mother is not noted for her tact, and she's desperate to see her grandchildren, but I think she's a darling and I hope you will too.' He laughed softly. 'Would you mind very much calling one of those children Hawke, to please her? We can make it a second name.'

Morna panicked. 'I don't know that I'd be any good as a mother.'

'From all accounts you brought yourself up,' he said promptly, the teasing inflection vanished from his voice. 'I'd say you're a brilliant mother. Now, can we take marriage for granted? I thought we might let Nick and Cathy know, and then this weekend we could fly down to tell my mother, and then you could start looking for a diamond the same colour as your eyes...'

He smoothed a finger along her eyebrow, and Morna looked up at him. 'You make it sound—easy.'

'My dearest heart,' he said deeply, holding her against him in an embrace that would always spell security. 'From now on I'll always try to make things easy for you. You'll object, and I'll be dictatorial, and sometimes we'll quarrel, but we love each other, so we can deal with anything that comes our way.'

His confidence convinced her. Sighing, she surrendered. 'Yes,' she whispered, and went into the strong haven of his arms.

EPILOGUE

MRS CHALLENGER got up and walked across to the window. 'Everything's going to be fine,' she announced to the other two people in the room.

In unison the Hardings said, 'Of course,' and Cathy added, 'Morna's as strong as a horse, and—'

The opening door interrupted her. The three inhabitants of the hospital waiting room pivoted as one and fixed the newcomer with pleading gazes.

Grinning, Hawke said, 'Everything's fine. She's great, and the babies are well and healthy, and heavy enough not to be classed as prems.'

The collective sigh made him laugh. 'She also said she's not ever going through this again.'

'She'll get over that,' Cathy said with a rueful sideways smile at her husband.

'Can we see her?' his mother asked.

'Give us half an hour or so, and then we'll all be ready for visitors.'

He left them exulting and went back to the sunny private ward where Morna had been wheeled with their children. As always his heart swelled when he saw her. She was lying in the bed with her damp hair clustering in tendrils around her face, a little pale but radiant, a supremely pleased smile curling her soft mouth. Tucked into a big crib beside the bed, sound asleep as befitted children who'd had a hard day, lay their son and daughter.

'Darling,' Morna said, her voice rich with happiness, and gave him the smile she reserved for him alone.

'Simon Hawke sucks his fist very noisily, but Fiona just closed her eyes and went to sleep. I hope they're going to be great friends with Penny.' Cathy and Nick's daughter was Morna's goddaughter.

Hawke bent to kiss each crumpled cheek, before sitting on the side of the bed to kiss his wife. She came easily into his arms, resting there with the confidence a year of marriage had given her.

'I love you,' he said.

She touched his mouth, whisky-golden eyes glowing with complete trust. 'Funny how love makes complete sense of everything,' she said peacefully. 'I feel as though I was put on the earth for this—to be your wife and their mother. And the best darned jeweller in the Southern Hemisphere.'

He smoothed the hair back from her brow. 'You don't regret giving up the shop, even though Annie's doing so well as manager?'

'I haven't given up anything, darling. I can still design and make pieces, and that wonderful workshop in our new house will keep my hand in until I stop being a full-time mother.'

They had built a house—glorious, open and sunny—at Tarika Bay. Hawke had paid off the debt she'd considered she owed to Glen, but he'd accepted her refusal to let him pay off the bank loan. He understood how she felt.

Against his lips she said, 'You've given me yourself, and your wonderful mother, not to mention that huge family of yours. And now the babies. You've given me the world.' A world she'd never known, never even hoped for.

Safe in each other's arms they watched their sleeping children, and their future spread out before them, glowing with the promise of a long and happy life filled with companionship and laughter and the security of their love.

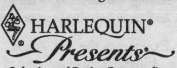

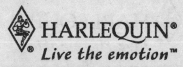

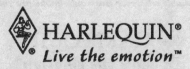

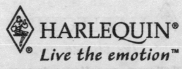

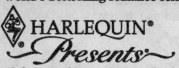

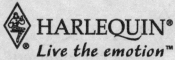

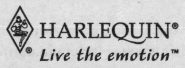